YOUNG MARINER

YOUNG MARINER

WALTER F. CURRAN

This book is a work of fiction. Names, characters, places and incidents are the product of the Author's imagination or are used fictitiously. Any resemblance to actual events, locales, or persons, living or dead, is coincidental

ISBN: 1530488419
ISBN 13: 9781530488414
Library of Congress Control Number: 2016904382
CreateSpace Independent Publishing Platform
North Charleston, South Carolina

CONTENTS

ACKNOWLEDGEMENTS

It was only after my trip to Ireland in June of 1996 that the writer within me flew free from his cage. A seminal event in my life because I discovered my heritage in Ireland and accepted that there was a more introspective and softer side of me than I had heretofore suspected or wanted.

I am blessed because I have accomplished just about everything I thought was possible for me to accomplish. Not that I've done great things, I haven't, but I believe I have met and perhaps slightly exceeded my own expectations.

It is not so much the great events in life that have inspired me as the individual efforts and achievements of ordinary people. Looking about, I am impressed by the man or woman that works hard to support, guide and set a good example for their children, abuses none of them and not only accepts but clings to this as a necessary part of life. That man or woman doing their daily grind are the backbone of my country and of many other countries throughout the world.

My wife Marie, son Christopher and daughter Amy with their respective spouses Brandy and Chris and wonderful grandchildren have been and continue to be my bedrock, but it is the legion of people I have worked with over the years that added the coloration and flavoring to my life and allowed me to view the world through their eyes. To them I say: Thank you! If, by chance, when reading this book, some of them feel a tinge of familiarity with a particular character, I assure it is pure imagination, just as it was mine that created the character.

Thanks to the other members of the Rehoboth Beach Writer's Guild Critique Group (Grey-head Club), Jackson Coppley, Frank Hopkins and Bill Kennedy whose insight, critiques and witticisms enhanced the book and enlivened my outlook. Thanks also to the Rehoboth Beach Writer's Guild for their overall support and the classes they offer to aspiring and established authors. The classes I attended were profoundly helpful. Special thanks to Michael McGowan for his fantastic efforts helping to design the cover of Young Mariner.

Last, but not least, I count myself as blessed I sailed with Moore McCormack Line when I graduated from Massachusetts Maritime Academy in 1966. A fantastic company to work for, I enjoyed every minute of my sailing time with them. Young Mariner is a work of fiction but many of the elements of the book, including how a commercial cargo ship operates were taken from my experiences when sailing as a deck officer. Wherever the name *MorMac* or *Pride* is used in this book, believe the good attributions. Anything bad is a figment of my overactive imagination.

Cover photos by Bill Vinson & Ginger Quering Casey

PROLOGUE

June 1966

Twelve hours clear of the Panama Canal, steaming northbound, heading for Brooklyn under an overcast sky not quite as gloomy as the two sitting in the captain's day room: Captain Coltrain and Chief Mate Dennis Hughes.

"What the bloody hell are we going to do now?" demanded the chief mate. "When I wired in for stores replenishment, that pompous ass in Marine Ops said they're taking us out of the Far East run and putting us back into the east coast of South America. He wouldn't even say why, just told me to plan accordingly. Dammit, Captain, this really screws the pooch."

"You need to calm down, Dennis. I admit, the change of route came a lot earlier than I expected. I thought we'd get at least two more runs in. We'll have to figure out what to do with the stuff. But there's no sense panicking. The pooch may be screwed, but it can still bark and bite. It isn't dead. For now, everything's closed up. We'll discuss this after we sail from Brooklyn and decide then what, if anything, we can salvage."

"Salvage my ass! We'd better worry about how we're gonna hide and dump this shit, not salvage it. If any of this is uncovered, we're all going away for a long time!"

"I said calm yourself, Dennis. Remember, we have business associates. We're not in this alone. What we do need to do is contact the sergeant and let him know there's going to be a delay. Use Sparky, but make damn sure you code the message. The last thing we want is Sparky sticking his nose into this."

"Don't worry about Sparky. He's nosy, but he's a pansy. If you look at him cross eyed, he starts to tear up. Besides, he thinks the sergeant is my cousin and we're talking about personal family stuff and that's the reason for the code. I'll send the wire tonight."

Chapter 1

THE CITY

There I was, William Connolly, signing in on a Friday night at the Seamen's Church Institute hotel in the Battery, Lower Manhattan, waiting to catch my first ship. Strange place for me to start, since I deemed myself to be retired from Catholicism. Still, it was cheap, clean, and, this being New York, as safe a place as I could hope to get with what I had to live on. Located at 25 South Street, the Seamen's Church Institute had opened in 1913, and it was definitely on its last legs.

Registration in the dank, somewhat worn-out lobby was a study in contrasts. The clerk was neatly dressed. The walls were dingy and dust covered. Hangings on the walls were well-cared-for religious artifacts conveying a sense of righteousness. Right next to the entrance to the small chapel was a rolling chalkboard with a handwritten notice: Thursdays—Alcoholics Anonymous Meetings in the Chapel. Adding to the contrast were the sordid-looking seamen of various nationalities, heavily scented of tobacco, beer, and wine, filling the lobby. Three of them, sitting on the couch under a large picture of Jesus dressed in a white robe, were dressed in a cacophony of colors.

I was shown to my room by a gnomish fellow with a beatific smile. The room was a cell by a normal person's standards and consisted of a bed, three-drawer dresser, nightstand with lamp and a Bible, and a rickety rail-back chair perfectly adequate for someone like me who had lived in close quarters on a ship for three years. The bathroom, however, was claustrophobic. Showing the gnome out, I unpacked, took a leak, and went back down to the lobby. I puttered through the various magazines and pamphlets while politely fending off an offer to attend chapel services.

I was starving but loath to spend any of my limited money on food. Finally, I broke down and bought chips and an Orange Crush from the canteen and settled into a comfortably worn chair in the common room. About an hour of watching TV was all I could take, so I went up to my room and stood staring out the window while pondering my immediate future.

Here I was on the threshold of the rest of my life, and I was excited. I was about to walk through the door labeled Financial Security, the ultimate goal for me since I was eight years old and barely able to even spell *finance*. As of this moment, I existed in that strange world between barely subsisting and well off. Having just graduated from Massachusetts Maritime Academy, I had the remains of my Maritime Administration subsidy and the couple hundred bucks I had managed to squirrel away over the past three years. Hardly what was needed to take on New York, but then again, I was just passing through. A transient in this city that was world famous for transients, I was about to become a highly paid third mate in the world's finest merchant marine.

I likened the whole thing to a religious transformation. I had just finished three years of hell, I was in limbo, and as soon as my ship was ready, I'd be in heaven. Anticipation continued to agitate my mind until sometime after midnight, when I hit the rack and drifted off.

The next morning, I phoned the steamship line office and talked with the marine superintendent, a short man of long Italian heritage known as Nunni, short for Nunzio. To some of the wiseasses down at the hiring hall, he was a jerk. But to a new junior third mate, he was God. I found out what I was supposed to do and when. Since I had nine days of limbo to contend with and a limited time to be on board the ship during dry-docking, I decided to use the time to get to know my way around New York.

I had already been in plenty of strange places on my training cruises, and I was raised in a big city—Boston—but New York intimidated me. It was just so damn big!

Stepping out into the mist and eschewing my nor'easter—*raincoat* to a landlubber—simply because I didn't want to go back to my room to get it, I meandered around until I found myself at Cortland Street Station. Studying the maps for a while, I thought, "It may be bigger, but it's laid out a lot more logically than the MTA, the Boston subway system." Finally, I took off into the subway.

I planned to surface at intersecting-route stations and look around just to see what the different neighborhoods were like. I even thought I might head out to the site of the 1964 World's Fair.

Growing up in Southie, a white, mostly Irish Catholic ghetto, you lived by the rules of and within the parameters of your neighborhood. If you weren't born and raised in the neighborhood, you were an outsider. We had Irish, Italians, Poles, Germans, and Lithuanians in our neighborhood, and we all got along. It wasn't the ethnicity so much as the outsider ideology that ruled our world. So as much as I was curious, I was also very cautious and keeping a low profile because I knew an outsider wouldn't be especially welcome in a strange neighborhood.

I decided one of the stops would be Yankee Stadium. An avid Yankees hater, I was still curious how the stadium compared to Fenway, home of the Red Sox. My tour was going along pretty well until I decided to get off at 125th Street to get a look at the Harlem River. When I came out to the street, I looked around and immediately started to get edgy. I had overlooked the fact that the Harlem River is in Harlem, and I was the only white face in sight. You can't keep a low profile under those conditions. In truth, the looks I got were more curious than hostile, but I obviously stood out and was nervous. So I turned around and dove back down into the subway, heading back to the Battery. That was the end of my neighborhood tour of New York.

I've never thought of myself as racist. Negroes were simply the most extreme example of outsiders because until very recently, there were no Negroes at all in Southie. There were a few Negroes in the projects, both Columbia Point and D Street, but Columbia Point was considered to be Dorchester by most folks from Southie. Everyone I knew referred to the D Street projects as the lower end and a fringe part of Southie. Until I was in high school, I never actually met and talked to a Negro. In high school, except for sports, everyone had their own clique. Mine was the guys from Southie.

I remember when I was about thirteen years old, the city completed the new causeway connecting the Sugarbowl to Castle Island. They created an artificial lagoon where it was always high tide. The official name was Pleasure Bay, but to us Southie kids it was "the lagoon." The original Sugarbowl was itself a causeway with a circular area at the end built to replace the covered walkway extending into the bay that was destroyed in the hurricane of 1938. It was a good fishing spot and a hangout at night, doubling as a "lovers' lane."

When the causeway was completed, the city promoted the new Pleasure Bay. Overnight, what used to be a private reserve for residents of City Point became a beach destination point for Bostonians from all over the city. It wasn't accepted well by locals.

Immediately, the road now known as Day Boulevard, named after Louise Day Hicks, a former city councilwoman, became a DMZ. Strangers, anyone not from Southie, were left alone if they stayed on the beach side of the road, but if they crossed over onto the land side, there was a better than fifty-fifty chance there would be a fight. The boulevard extended almost three miles from the Columbia Point projects, past Carson Beach, the L Street bathhouses, M Street Beach, and Kelly's Landing down to Castle Island.

One day in July, a half dozen guys from Dorchester, four white and two black, came across the street in front of Kelly's Landing. They started making comments about the girlfriends of two Southie guys. The Southie guys did what we all did back then. They started throwing punches. For a couple of minutes, the six were beating up on the two, but then the boys from City Point arrived, fifteen of them, and the Dorchester guys took off running in the direction of the Columbia Point projects with a mob chasing them.

Another ten or so guys jumped into cars and got ahead of them and intercepted them just past the L Street bathhouse. If the cops from Station Six hadn't shown up just as everyone was putting the boots to them, I don't think they would have survived.

When I got back to the Seamen's Church Institute, I felt both humiliated and embarrassed: the former because I had run away from Harlem on the strength of my innate fears and suspicions, and the latter because, although I was the only one who knew what had happened back then, I felt as if I had a poster hanging over me that said "Racist!" It's strange the effect that embarrassment has on your mind, a weird blend of resentment, hostility, and guilt. I made a point out of going up to the only Negro I had seen at the SCI at the time, an older guy around forty or so about my height, five foot eleven, trim with mahogany skin. I blurted out, "Are you a seaman?"

"Yeah," he said. "I been here for about a week waiting to meet my ship."

"Do you mind if I ask you a question?"

"Shoot," he replied.

"What do you suppose would happen if a white person just started to walk around Harlem by themselves? Do you think they'd be in trouble?"

To my ever-loving surprise, he just laughed and said, "Hell, man, I don't know! I never been there myself because I heard it was such a rough part of town."

It took a bit to sink in, but this was another important object lesson in learning not to assume. I had assumed that because he was a Negro and he was staying at the Seamen's Church Institute, he knew all about Harlem. Big mistake!

I stuttered and stammered through a conversation in which he told me he was a native of Baltimore, had just attended a funeral at home, and only happened to be in New York because this was where his ship was due to dock. Having elicited all this from him, I realized I didn't even know his name and hadn't told him mine. This far into the conversation, I was too embarrassed to ask. As much as I had traveled, I was still quite shy, naïve, and awkward when it came to dealing with strangers. Now doubly embarrassed, I thanked him and left as he stared at me with a sort of bemused half grin.

Chapter 2

ANXIETY

I woke up before the alarm went off, which was rare. Ever since I had escaped reveille at school, I had treated sleep like a long-lost friend and any artificial means of waking as the enemy. Splashing cold water on my face, I got dressed and went down to the canteen for coffee. Mind you, I didn't really like coffee, but it was effective in keeping me awake on night watches.

Lighting up a Marlboro, I poured my coffee from the mug into a cardboard cup and walked outside. It was cool for June, and it felt good. As I stood on the edge of the curb, still as a fire hydrant, absorbing the sights, sounds, and smells of the Battery waking up, it hit me like a ton of bricks. That anxious wave passed over me, the prelude to a "spell."

At age ten, I woke up in the middle of the night sobbing piteously. My ma came in and asked me what was wrong. "Grandpa died from a sore lip," I blurted out. Smiling gently as only a ma can do, she patted me and said, "Grandpa didn't die. You had a nightmare. It's okay now." That weekend, we learned that Grandpa had cancer of the throat and mouth. He died from it within a year. My ma treated me a little differently from then on. I don't think she ever told anyone else though. If my sisters had known, they would have ragged on me big time.

Since then, I'd had a number of these déjà vu types of incidents, and most of them were preceded by a horrible feeling of anxiety and fear, where I would feel like I was on fire, pouring sweat and shivering all at the same time. I referred to them as spells, and occasionally, I would get a spell without the déjà vu. In the last two years, they had reduced in number and intensity but hadn't stopped completely. Having never talked to a doctor about it, I didn't know if there was a medicine for this condition. But since it was lessening, I was simply riding it out.

This time, it passed before it flared into the full-blown feeling of panicked fear that always shook me to the core. It was frustrating, perplexing, and scary, and I never knew what would trigger it. I suspected that certain smells triggered it, since smells, more than sights or sounds, have such a direct connection to memory.

At times like these, all I wanted to do was retreat and hide, wary of human contact. In a single breath, New York went from an adventure to a terrifying prison!

I knew it would pass. It always passed, but that didn't stop me from being frozen in time with the feeling. Even an instant was too long for me. Intellect doesn't always win out over emotion.

Gradually coming back to the here and now, breaths beginning to elongate from truncated gasps, I realized I had dropped my cigarette into the gutter and squeezed the cup so hard it had ruptured. Coffee was all over my pants and shoes. Teetering backward all the way to the building, I leaned on it, taking deep breaths, and felt control slowly starting to return.

Looking around, acutely aware now of my demeanor, I tried to appear casual and see if anyone had noticed. But this was New York, and no one was even looking in my direction. If they had noticed, they weren't showing any interest. Classic New Yorker aloofness. Standing up straight, testing to make sure my balance was intact, I walked back inside and went right up to my room and lay down. As usual, once the initial feeling passed, I became both introspective and angry: angry that anything could wrest control away from me the way the spell did and introspective because many times this was the precursor to déjà vu, which was even scarier.

When nothing else happened after half an hour, I sat up and began mentally retreating, convincing myself that if I didn't think about it, it wouldn't be there.

It was also always after incidents like these that I began to have second thoughts about my cynical outlook toward religion. On one hand, I wanted to thank God that the spell had passed. On the other hand, I wanted to blame God, as if he had afflicted me with some sort of voodoo curse. And then there was a third, invisible hand that usually slapped me in the face and said, "Knock off this God nonsense!"

I am of two minds when it comes to religion. Not Catholicism, but religion. I had long ago made up my mind that priests and, to a lesser extent, nuns, were simply a better class of hypocrites than most others on earth. No, I'm talking about pure religion—no trappings, rituals, or rites—simply where a man talks directly to God looking for some kind of guidance on whatever the topic happens to be at the time. Most times, I found myself talking only to myself, and I already knew that I didn't know the answer to whatever the question was. Inane, yes, but somehow logical.

As usual after a spell hits me, my brain was hyperactive, thoughts chasing wildly around inside my skull. I started a routine I had used in the past with word games and rhyming as a distraction. I ultimately resorted to a half-assed meditation I had taught myself. Managing to slow my thoughts down to a reasonable pace, I faded out.

When I again became aware of the room around me, I looked at the clock and was astounded to see that it was after 5:00 p.m. Taking another basin bath, I changed out of my coffee-stained pants, wiped off and polished my shoes—some habits die hard—and went down to the lobby.

There were a lot of guys milling around, including the Negro I had talked to yesterday. He nodded at me but didn't say anything, and I returned the nod. He wasn't smiling today, but I still had the feeling he found me pretty amusing.

Hunger pangs hit, and I realized that I hadn't had a real meal since yesterday's breakfast. Remembering there was a food wagon a half block down toward Battery Park, and hoping it was open at this time, I went and reluctantly spent some money for food. I bought a hamburger and french fries and even bought a Table Talk blueberry pie to take back to the room for dessert.

I lay in my rack for a few hours listening to my sister's portable Zenith that I had inherited from her and allowed myself the luxury of thinking about Muriel, my on-again-off-again girlfriend. It was really the only cloud on my horizon, the fact that I had to leave her for so long. It's not as if we had made any serious commitments to each other, but she was a lot of fun, and I missed her. The last time we were together was at the Cape, and it had been earthshaking for me.

We had arrived at the small, sheltered cove around 10:00 a.m., and, aside from a short walk to a lone vendor selling bottles of juice and tonic from a cooler, we had been completely absorbed in one another.

The sun was setting, but it was still warm. We were the last ones left. The only other couple had walked back behind the dunes about twenty minutes earlier and had taken their blanket and things with them, so they weren't coming back. We had frolicked in and out of the water all day and couldn't remember being so happy.

She lay facedown on the blanket, having undone her bikini top for the third time that day in order to minimize the tan line. Each time she did, I would see more of the swell of her breast, and each time I had to mentally talk myself into calming down. Lying there beside her, I asked, "Did you have a good time today?"

"Uh-huh," she murmured.

Propping myself up on my right elbow, I slowly reached out with my left hand and, ever so gently, traced my fingers down the center ridge of her back. As I did, she emitted a slight shiver and sighed. Slowly, lovingly, up and down her spine, gently increasing the pressure each time from a tickle to a massage, higher and lower with each pass. Starting at her neck, I pressed and splayed my fingers around the nape and then skied down the ridgeline of her spine, slowly inching into the line of her bikini bottom, teasing the crease of her buttocks.

At last, she turned over on her back, exposing her breasts. Reaching out to my cheek, she caressed me, gave an impish yet beatific smile, and said, "That side's done." This was new territory. We had kissed, and I had felt her up before, but we were clearly stepping over a threshold.

Leaning down, I kissed her. It was a gentle, delicate probing and flicking of tongues but soon evolved into a jousting match, stabbing and darting. We'd kissed many times, but the passion was so much more intense. I was so aroused that it was almost painful. At the same time my tongue drifted from her lips to her nipple, her hand slid into my bathing suit and found me, and the quivering intensified.

Arching her hips, she pushed down her bikini bottom. I immediately wriggled out of my bathing suit. Pushing me onto my back, she leaned down and flicked the end of my penis once with her tongue. More than once would have been the end for me. Again showing that impish smile, she glided up over me, slowly impaling herself. For the longest time, she just lay there, not moving, almost purring, and then arching her back, she said, "Lick my nipples," and thrust hard with her hips. It didn't last long, but it was the most intense pleasure I had ever felt. In retrospect, I don't know if she had an orgasm or not. I was too new at it to tell and too excited to care.

Later, as we lay beside each other, she lifted up, stared deeply into my eyes, and said, "Where did you learn to be so gentle?"

"I was afraid I'd hurt you. I'm old fashioned. Never hurt a lady."

"What if I had rolled over and told you to stop?"

"I would have stopped. I probably would have had to pole-vault my way down the beach, but I would have stopped."

She laughed. "I wouldn't want you to hurt yourself pole-vaulting. My way was better." Staring into my eyes, she said, "I think I love you. I'm not really sure, but I think so."

After a while, I tuned out the thought of her and eventually drifted off to the sound of the Beatles playing their ballad "Michelle."

While in Baltimore, Greg was reminded of the past, many parts of which, due to his age and travels, he now saw in a different light—a harsher, disappointing glare.

Born in Columbus, Ohio, Greg had moved with his family to Baltimore in 1950, moving into the west side of the city, a predominantly Negro area. He was happy enough during his formative years, growing up in a mostly Negro neighborhood but attending an integrated school system. His mother, a housewife, and father, a school janitor, both strict Baptists, inserted their moral values deeply into his psyche, and he had developed a strong sense of right and wrong, something that had manifested itself throughout his life. He also had a highly developed sense of tolerance. This too was instilled from his parents, mainly his father, as a means of dealing with the blatant racism that he encountered as he slowly maneuvered his way into the white man's world. He recalled his father's infinite patience as he explained to him that in order to overcome racism, you had to get to really know someone. Once a man saw you for what you really were, the color faded. He also taught Greg that racism was a two-way street. Don't expect others to adapt and change if you won't. The real reason he was bummed out, other than the loss of Granny, someone who had always doted on him, typically sneaking little treats to him in a grand conspiracy against his parents, was that his father, once a bastion of reasonableness, at least in Greg's mind, had become old and bitter, seemingly overnight. His mother's way of coping with this was to become a recluse. When he told them he was returning to the ship, he got a tepid hug from his mother, but his father never came out of his room.

Sitting by himself in the lobby, Greg roused from his reverie and looked up just as the white guy he ran into yesterday was crossing the lobby and heading toward the door. Given that he was so obviously uncomfortable talking to him, he thought he'd go right by. But after a slight hesitation, he came over, stuck out his hand, and introduced himself. Strange boy! Not predictable at all. It turned out he was heading for the *Pride* also, so I suggested we share a cab. Again, that slight hesitation, and I wondered if he was thinking, "Don't get too close to him." Maybe he's one of those rednecks that think the color rubs off. Who knows? Anyway, he finally agreed, so I grabbed my briefcase, and we headed out.

Up at 0600 sharp. Today I would actually report to the ship and look it over. I wouldn't be signing articles until later in the week. Articles are officially a contract between the steamship line and the individual crew member outlining the approximate length of the voyage, the position in which you are employed, and the general conditions under which you will live. Nunzio, the marine superintendent, had strongly suggested I get off on a good footing with the captain, who epitomized the old cliché "He'll eat you for breakfast without even a burp."

Too nervous to eat, I had a pint of milk, gathered my papers, and went to the lobby.

My plan was to follow the intricacies of the subway over to Todd's Ferry, having mapped it out when I was touring. As luck would have it, the same Negro I had run into the day before was waiting by the door, and since I couldn't avoid him without looking like I was trying to, I stepped up and said, "Hi! I never got your name the other day."

Coolly, with a hint of that smirk I was beginning to find very annoying, he stuck out his hand and said, "Greg Russell. What's yours?"

"William Connolly," I replied.

After an awkward—at least for me—silence, I continued.

"You said you were waiting for a ship. What one?"

To my astonishment, he said, "I'm joining the *Mormacpride*."

"That's the ship I'm waiting for. In fact, I'm on my way down to Todd's Ferry right now to meet the captain."

"How are you getting there?"

"I was planning on taking the subway."

"Don't do that. It takes forever. Let's split a cab."

Slight hesitation as the cash register in my head sounded. Then I said, "That's fine." Greg picked up his briefcase from a table in the corner, and we walked out and hailed a cab.

After telling the driver where to go, Greg turned to me.

"You must be one of the third mates. I heard they were changing both of them again. I'm the third engineer. I've been here awhile now. Most of the crew are homesteaders. Until now, except for the third mates, I was the newest man on the entire ship."

"What do you mean, except for the third mates?" I asked.

He gave me a serious "Are you shitting me?" look.

"You really don't know about Captain Coltrain's reputation?"

"Well, Nunzio did say that he eats third mates for breakfast, but I figured that was the usual spiel they give new third mates. You know, make sure you watch your p's and q's."

"William, I hate to tell you, but in this case, old Nunzio was not exaggerating. No one can even remember when a third mate made back-to-back trips!"

After a pause, he continued.

"It isn't just young guys either. He's been roughest on some of the old mates. It seems he holds them to a higher standard. I don't pretend to understand why, and I'm sure as hell not going to ask him why. I'm just glad he leaves the Engine Department alone. He only bothers the chief, and Bill seems to be able to handle it okay."

"Jeez! You make it sound like the Marquis de Sade!"

"Well, I'm just glad I'm not a deckie." He chuckled.

"It isn't funny, you know! I plan on making this a career, and you're telling me that I'm starting out on a ship run by the captain from hell! Christ, what a way to start!"

In a more serious tone, trying to calm me down, he said, "Look at it this way. If you quit at the end of the trip, you'll be only one of a long line of third mates. At least they can't single you out for not staying with him."

I didn't respond, just stared out the window of the cab at what seemed to me to be frenetic activity but was probably normal for New York City.

I was astonished at Greg's candor and the fact that he was the third engineer. Once again, my presumptive prowess, due mainly to stereotypical input, had failed miserably. I thought he was a seaman, one of the unlicensed crew. Trying to ease back into conversation, I asked, "What's a homesteader?" I had never heard that term, at least in relation to ships.

He laughed and said, "That's anyone who stays on the same ship all the time. Generally, they only get off for vacation and then wait for the ship to return to sign on again."

I don't know why, but I had always thought that everyone except for maybe the captain and chief engineer changed ships at the end of every trip.

He went on to explain that he had gotten permission to sign off in Panama and fly home for his grandmother's funeral. He was entitled to take vacation but hadn't planned on it and didn't want to hang around in what was a palling atmosphere at home.

The cab wound its way through Brooklyn and finally dropped us just outside the gate to the shipyard. Greg led the way as we walked down to the ship. As we were crossing the shipyard gangway, he stopped.

Turning to me, he said, "A word to the wise. The engineers on here are good guys, good at their job and easy to get along with. So is the mate. The captain is a stuck-up prick! I don't like him, and neither do any of the other engineers. They all make fun of him behind his back. The chief engineer says the main office loves him because he keeps a good schedule and rarely has any problems in port. You're new, and as I've already told you, he loves to chew on third mates, so watch your ass."

He started to turn away. Then, touching my arm, he continued, "The flip side to that is, if any third mate lasts more than one trip with him, it would mean he likes them and would probably recommend them to the main office. But before you get too excited, keep in mind this is my fourth trip and there's been new third mates every trip."

With that piece of dubious encouragement, I watched him turn and step onto the deck, sign in with the watchman, and walk forward. Just as he reached the companionway door, he turned back to me.

"If you're going back to the Seamen's Center, leave word with the gangway watchman, and we can go back together."

With that, he stepped over the coaming and disappeared.

Standing on the brow gangway, I had a good profile view of the ship. The *Mormacpride* was a general cargo ship built for Moore McCormack Lines to use primarily in the Great Lakes trade. Known as a 1624, she was a C-3-class ship built specifically for the trade routes known to MorMac as routes 1, 16, and 24. She was 483 feet 3 inches length over all (LOA), with a 68-foot beam, weighing 9,252 gross tons. She was launched February 1, 1960, at the Sun Ship Building & Dry Dock Company in Chester, Pennsylvania. With five cargo hatches using conventional booms/derricks as well as a heavy lift boom that could be swung between hatches two and three, she was a workhorse. They also built in accommodations for up to twelve passengers and a postage-stamp-size swimming pool behind the bridge. Twin steam turbines linked to one propeller shaft generated 12,100 horsepower, so she could do twenty-one knots in calm weather. Standing there, looking at the smokestack insignia, a green background with a white circle and a large red *M* in the middle, I felt the beginnings of a sense of belonging.

Stepping onto the deck, I signed in and asked the watchman where the captain was located. He pointed at the same door that Greg went through and said, "In there and up three decks." I thanked him, walked forward, and entered the crew's quarters.

The most immediate sensation was smell, a mélange of odors. Only a skeleton crew was actually living on board at the time, but they had electric power, and they obviously were cooking their meals on board. I stepped over the high sill. All the doors were the watertight variety. I went in and started climbing the ladders, went past the engineers' deck, then the mates' deck, and finally reached the captain's stateroom and lounge deck. The owner's cabin and passenger cabins were also here, just below the bridge deck.

Taking a deep breath, I started toward the lounge but stopped for a moment when I noticed that the licenses were all posted on the bulkhead. Quickly peeking at the names, I was surprised to recognize the name of one of the engineers: Patrick Fahey. He was posted in the third's position but had a first engineer's license. If it was the same Fahey I knew, he had been one of my upper jobs. That's a first classman when I was a freshman. Freshmen were derogatively referred to as youngies. Fahey had been a smartass, but not really a bad guy.

Continuing on my way, I knocked on the open stateroom door, and a nasally, reedy voice called out, "Yeahas," in a very snooty-like voice. I stepped in, and there was no one there.

Looking around, I realized there was an open connecting door between the captain's stateroom and what appeared to be the captain's bedroom. So I said, "Good morning, Captain Coltrain. My name is Connolly, and I'm the new junior third mate."

I stood there for what seemed like forever before the captain made his entrance. And that's exactly what it was: an entrance. He came sauntering in from his room. It was all I could do to keep from laughing. He was dressed like a Hollywood star. Slippers, silk smoking jacket, long cigarette holder complete with a brand I later found out to be a Dunhill. He had an affected air that you could cut with a knife. Standing at least six foot four in his slippers, he looked amazingly like Peter O'Toole.

After staring at me for what seemed like forever, he smiled, came close to me, and said, "What makes you think you're the junior third mate on my ship?" stressing the *my* heavily.

"Oh shit!" I thought. "Here we go! What am I getting into here?"

I managed to stammer, "Captain, the marine superintendent at the main office assigned me here, and I picked up the assignment slip at the hall."

Again, he took an inordinately long time and finally said, "Sit down, and let's talk."

As soon as my butt touched the seat, he barked, "Sonny!"

I snapped to a sitting attention. I soon got used to this because it was the only way he ever addressed either of the third mates unless he was pissed off. Then he would roar out, "Mr. Connolly!" and you knew immediately that another piece of your ass was about to get bitten off.

Taking a seat he resumed, "Sonny, Nunzio is a very nice gentleman. The union hall has its rules regarding hiring, and they send me officers they recommend. But remember, first and foremost, this is *my* ship and *I* am the only one who decides who stays and who goes. If you understand that, we can continue. If you don't, you can leave right now!"

Stunned, I manage to stammer, "I understand, Captain."

"Good," he said. "Do you have any questions?"

I paused for a second and then replied, "Yes, sir. When do I officially report, and do you want me to do anything in particular right now?"

"Good questions," he pronounced. "We'll be signing articles on Friday, and we're scheduled to sail next Monday. You should report on Thursday. The ship will be afloat by then, and we'll have it in full operation. For now, I suggest you find Mr. Hughes, the chief mate, and report to him."

He stood, and I instinctively leaped to my feet. Without a word, he turned and walked back to his room. As he disappeared through the door, he paused and without turning around, spoke over his shoulder.

"So far, so good, sonny. Remember, there are two answers to any question that I ask. 'Yes, Captain,' and 'I don't know, Captain.' Anything you don't know, you better find out about damn quick."

The exit was as grand as the entrance, and again I thought, "This is pure theatrics." But it still didn't stop my ass from puckering!

By now, I was thoroughly intimidated. I stepped back into the passageway, my mind going a thousand miles an hour.

"What have I gotten myself into? I thought all the hazing crap was over. Is this just a new, enhanced level of hazing?"

Going below, I went to the mate's room and knocked on the door. There was no answer. Knowing full well that asking the captain where the mate was wasn't a viable option, I decided I'd just look around until I found him myself. While I searched, the object of my quest sat with the chief engineer in the chief's stateroom.

The two sitting there were polar opposites in looks. The chief mate was a shade over six feet tall, and the chief engineer was barely five foot five. The mate had a chunky build with large love handles that billowed the bottom of his shirt. The chief was neat and trim, a long-distance runner's body. The mate had a pasty complexion and a really bad comb-over of mousy brown hair with obvious bald spots. The chief had a dark brown crew cut, and his face was tanned, as were his arms where they were exposed below his rolled-up jumpsuit sleeves.

"When do you think we'll get a chance to get in there, Dennis?" Bill, the chief engineer, asked. "Other than the consigned stuff, I'm not even sure what's there because it carried over from two trips."

"Yeah, Bill. I know. It's a ton of stuff, and I don't have the foggiest idea when we'll get to it. Even after we get it out, I don't know what we can do with it. Without hitting Balboa, there's no way to unload the stuff. Maybe we should just sit tight and sweat it out. This is just a temporary routing. They might change us back over again after this trip. The machines and beer are dispensable. If we have to dump them, we dump them. But I'm not dumping the guns until I abso-fuckin'-lutely know there's no other way to handle it. That's part of my retirement fund."

"Retirement? If we get caught, you'll be retired all right. But you ain't gonna like your bunkies! Besides, who said anything about dumping it? I admit that was my first thought, but we still have our Pacific partners to deal with. This isn't like the other cash-and-carry deals, you know. This is big bucks! The sarge said one of their friends would contact us here, but we haven't heard anything yet."

"I'm beginning to get a bad feeling about this, Bill. The other stuff was pretty simple, and there weren't many people involved. We don't know who these friends of Sarge are, and the stuff we're carrying this time is a little more volatile than before. I don't think anyone even gives a shit about the beer and sewing machines because they probably don't even know they're missing, what with the lousy bookkeeping they have. But when you move guns, well, that's a different story. Every gun is supposed to be registered and traceable."

"Yeah, I wasn't too happy with it either when Sarge proposed it, but in for a penny, in for a dollar. I figured most of the risk was on Sarge's side, because whoever picks it up has to run the gauntlet and get it off the pier."

Interrupted by a knock at the door, the chief engineer held up his hand and said, "Come in."

After wandering around for ten minutes looking for the mate, I went to the gangway watchman, and he suggested I try the chief engineer's room. That's where I found him.

On most merchant ships, the chief mate is commonly referred to as Mate. All other deck officers are called by their rank, either second or third. It's similar with the engineers, with the chief engineer being called Chief, and all others by their rank, either first, second, or third.

When I entered, they both looked up, and after a short pause, the mate said, "I can tell by that leery, somewhat dazed look on your face that you've already met Captain Coltrain." Both he and the chief snorted a laugh.

"It's okay," he said. "You're not the first third mate to go into shock. We've even had a few that just left and were never heard from again!"

At this they both broke out laughing again. Finally, the mate stood, offered his hand, and said, "Welcome aboard. Which one are you? Connolly or Adams?"

"I'm William Connolly, sir."

"Well, it's good to meet you, William. Or is it Bill?"

"I prefer William, sir."

Turning toward the other guy, he said, "This is our chief engineer, Bill Bradley," with the emphasis on the *Bill*.

"Oh shit," I thought. "They probably think I'm a snotnose because I don't like to be called Bill." That sinking feeling was coming back in a hurry.

The chief saved the situation, saying, "Don't let these guys bother you. I wanted them to call me William too, but they're too damned insubordinate. So I was forced to tolerate them."

I shot him a look that clearly said, "I owe you one."

"Have a seat," the chief said. "Do you want coffee?"

"No, thanks, Chief."

The mate said, "I'm Dennis Hughes. Since you met the captain, you already know who God is. The rest of us are mere mortals who do his bidding." Having said that, he looked at me sort of quizzically, giving me a long stare, and asked, "Are you a wise ass?"

"What do you mean?" I responded, instantly defensive.

"Just what I said. Are you a wise ass?"

After a few seconds, I said, "No. I'm not."

"Good," he rattled. "We got that settled. The reason I asked is because we have a real good crew on this ship, mostly homesteaders, and we want to keep it that way. We welcome folks with a sense of humor. Notwithstanding our comments about the captain, we treat each other with respect, and there's very little trouble on board. As for the captain, we kid about his mannerisms, but understand, he's one of the best in the fleet, if not the best. We don't particularly like him, but we very much respect his abilities. Another thing, you haven't earned the right to say anything about the captain. You might in time if you survive, but not yet. Understand?"

"Yes, sir."

"Good. Let's take a walk around, and you can get acquainted with the ship."

I said good-bye to the chief and followed the mate below.

"We'll be here in the yard until at least Saturday" he said. "We weren't even scheduled for this, but they took us off-charter to the government, and it left a hole in the schedule. So they decided to do the annual inspection and also fix the steering problems and a few other problems we've had.

"We've been running to 'Nam and Thailand, and we were all expecting to just turn around and head back out there again. The change is a pain in the ass, but we'll cope with it."

I asked him why it was such a problem to change runs, and he stopped, looked at me closely, harrumphed, and walked on without answering.

By this time, we were back in the unlicensed crew's quarters, and the mate knocked on a door labeled Boatswain that was partly ajar and called out, "Hey, Boats!"

From within a response came, "Comin', Mate."

After a few seconds, Boats came out. A tall man, about six foot three, he had a beer gut, a ruddy face that had seen a few too many fists, and hands that looked like small boulders and felt like rough-cut four-by-fours when he reached out to shake hands with me.

"Boats, I'd like you to take Mr. Connolly here on a tour of the Deck Department and show him the general layout."

"Okay, Mate," Boats said. Then, turning to me, he said, "C'mon, I'll show ya the good half of the ship."

And off he went in what seemed to me to be an abnormally long stride. I was practically trotting along behind him, trying to keep up.

Chapter 3

FIRST POLITICS

Boats headed toward the bow, ducked behind the ladder leading up to the mooring station, and went into a locker in the fo'c'sle.

"This here's my office," he offered in a nasal twang that was hard to place. "I do all my business from here. Unless it's an emergency, no one knocks on my door 'ceptin' the mate. Even the cap'n don't bother me there. You ever been to sea before?" he asked.

"Just on the training-ship cruises."

"What school?"

"Mass Maritime."

"Well," he said, smirking, "there may be hope for ya. We got us a couple of other Mass boys on board. Course, they're snipes, but still, not too bad. The one thing you Mass boys got over most of the other schoolboys is ya know how to live in tight quarters. What I was saying about not knocking on my room, it ain't like I'm bein' highfalutin' or nothin'. It's privacy. Ya learn to really 'preciate privacy on a ship."

"Yeah, Boats. That I do appreciate."

Looking around the locker, he said, "Siddown. Let's talk."

The most convenient seat was on a pallet of five-gallon buckets of paint, so I hitched up on it and looked at him, waiting for him to begin.

"This is a good ship and a good crew."

I began to think that everybody started their day by saying, "This is a good ship and crew." It was fast becoming a mantra.

"Most of us have been with her since she came out of the yard. Kind of like family, ya know? If ya got problems, ya keep it in the family. It's nobody's business but ours, understand?"

He was staring hard at me all the while he was talking. I nodded.

"So this is the way it works. The cap'n stays on the bridge and keeps his distance. The mate and I run the ship. I keep things quiet and shipshape. I fix any problems. The mate keeps the cap'n happy, and the cap'n keeps the company happy. It's real simple so long as everyone remembers: any problems, see me first."

"Boats, I read you loud and clear. This is my first trip, and I'm not about to rock the boat."

"Good," he said, standing up and stretching. "The scuttlebutt is that we'll set sea watches Friday at eighteen hundred hours. Until then, everyone is on day work. Once I see what watch you've got, I'll talk to the AB and ordinary and make sure they don't act up. New thirds are fair game for the usual bullshit, but it don't get out of hand.

"If I was you, I'd take a good look at all the hatches, how the covers work, and find all the sounding tubes. That's the mate's hang-up. The tubes are partly exposed in the lower holds, and he's always expectin' them to be blocked or crimped so's he won't get true soundin's." Sounding tubes are pipes that run from the main deck down to the holds, tanks, and bilges of the ship. They are used to measure whether or not there is any liquid in those areas, and if so, how much.

I stood there at the door of the fo'c'sle locker while Boats walked down the port side aft into the house. Stepping out, I saw that number two hold was directly in front of me, so I climbed down the ladder and started my tour. The cargo holds are numbered sequentially starting with number one at the bow and working aft to number five. The forward-most hold, number one, has a small work area in the lower hold due to the sheer of the ship. Sheer is the curvature of the bow that allows the ship to cut through the water more easily. As you travel aft, the hull widens, and the shape of the hold becomes more box-like until you reach number five, where the hull curves inward in a smooth curve toward the rudder and propeller. This reduces cargo storage space similar to number one hold.

I was coming out of the manhole at number four hatch, a watertight opening at the top of the hatch directly above the ladder leading down into the hatch. It is similar to emerging from a manhole over a sewer in the street. The mate, standing at the opening on the main deck leading to the house, called out, "Hey, William! Coffee break!" and then walked back into the house. Since I didn't have my own room yet, I used the head in the pilot's cabin behind the bridge to wash up. It's called a pilot's cabin but is used by anyone that needs to be near the bridge while the ship is underway. It provides a convenient head and a bunk for catnaps. I then went into the officers' salon for a cup of coffee.

"Dennis, those shipyard clowns have been all over the holds, supposedly inspecting for leaks. But they're looking at every weld and seam to see if they can generate more repair business. So far, they've looked below it and above it, but they don't seem to be looking right at it. It's only a matter of time before they do, and they might start asking questions about the welds in the middle of what is supposed to be a solid sheet of steel. I don't want it to reach that point. Do you understand? Find some excuse to close up the hold and keep it closed. I want you to personally check it!"

Sighing, the mate nodded, saying, "Sure thing, Captain."

"Another thing, Dennis. I want you to back off on Sparky."

"Is he crying to you again? Hell, nobody's bothered him for weeks that I know of."

"No, it isn't anything specific. I just don't want him getting too upset."

Looking straight at him, Dennis asked, "What's going on, Captain? You never gave a rat's ass about Sparky before. In fact, if I recall correctly, you thought that the fire ants in his knapsack were justified for the messages that he lost last month."

Chuckling, the captain replied, "That's true. It was quite a sight to see him jumping around and swatting at himself, especially when he hit himself in the cojones with the magazine. Nevertheless, ask the guys to back off. I have my reasons."

"Okay, I'll tell them, but I can't guarantee anything if Sparky starts pulling his lost-messages shit again."

"Just tell them," he insisted.

Reflecting on his last directive to the chief mate, the captain knew that if Sparky got pissed off enough at the officers, he may possibly upset their little smuggling applecart, and he didn't want to take any chances.

As I walked in, I saw the mate off at a corner table with the captain. They were both leaning over, looking at what appeared to be ship's drawings. I walked over to the sideboard, poured myself a cup of coffee, and heard the captain say to the mate, "I want you to personally check it."

The mate seemed to shrug but said, "Sure thing, Captain."

Standing upright, the captain turned and, spotting me, folded the drawings and handed them to the mate. As if hitting a switch, his composure changed from serious to Hollywood aristocrat. Pulling out a cigarette and inserting it into the holder, he drawled, "Well, sonny, how do you like my ship?"

"I like it just fine, Captain," I said, having already decided that the less said to the captain, the better.

"Good. Learn her well, and she won't surprise you."

He turned and left the officers' salon, and I could feel a collective exhale as the others in the room relaxed. The salon was amidships in the house, with square ports facing forward allowing plenty of natural light. There were four square tables for the officers and two round tables for the passengers. The captain usually sat at one of the round tables. The scullery was on the starboard side, and all of the food came up from the galley on the main deck via a dumbwaiter. There was a TV up high in the aft port corner and bookshelves under the TV.

Besides the mate and myself, scattered around the tables were the third engineer, Greg Russell; the chief, Bill Bradley; and the first and second engineers, both of whom were recognizable by their insignias and the grease on their coveralls.

Greg gave me a half wave and called out to the first engineer.

"Mark, this is the new third mate I was telling you about. William, meet Mark Quigley, our first engineer. Sitting next to him is Roy Oliver, the second engineer."

I walked up to them, extended a hand, and said, "Hello."

Mark was six feet two inches tall, weighed in at about 220 pounds, and had a mop of chestnut hair that looked like it was combed with a hand grenade. He smiled and simply said, "Welcome aboard," as we shook hands. Mark's hands seemed small and delicate for someone his size.

Roy Oliver was a whole different story. He stood about six feet even, weighed maybe 180 pounds, had thin, light brown hair and hawklike facial features, and exuded attitude.

He stared at my hand without taking it and remarked in a deep southern drawl, "Ya know, if you had any sense at all, you'd leave now while the gettin's good. The cap'n will eat you up! Y'all won't find no stiff necks like that in the Engine Department."

Although taken aback, I recovered quickly, and again extending my hand to him, I said, "It's a pleasure to meet someone so quiet and reserved. You be sure and let me know when you're going to offer an opinion on something, because I sure wouldn't want to miss it."

With that, he let out a bellow that startled me until I realized it was his peculiar way of laughing. The entire room started picking on him, and the chief said, "Ho, Roy, I think you met your match."

"Not likely," he snorted. But he was smiling, and it looked sincere.

Beckoning with his index finger, which was unusually long, he slapped the table in front of him and said, "Come on and sit down, boy."

I turned back to the sideboard and picked up the coffee I had set down when the intros began and sat down where Roy indicated.

"Where y'all from, boy?" he asked.

"Southie. South Boston."

"Sheeit!" he exclaimed. "We got ourselves another Yankee." Turning to the first, he said, "Y'all promised me that y'all wouldn't drag down no more Yankees." Turning back to me, he said, "What school ya from?"

"Mass Maritime."

"I knew it!" he roared. "This is a goddamn conspiracy! Y'all did this on purpose, didn't ya?" he accused the first engineer.

The first, for his part, pretended like nothing at all was happening and no one was addressing him. Finally, after what was an uncomfortable period of silence, the first turned, looked Roy straight in the eye, and said quietly, "Fuck you, Roy!"

The entire room broke up. I thought the chief would have a heart attack he was laughing so hard, and Roy was laughing right along with them.

"All right, boy, now we got that over with, I'll tell ya how it really is around here. We do a lot of poking fun at one another, but it's just that: fun. Ya can't take the funnin' serious, and ya can't get mad at anyone over it. The fact that you're a Mass boy is good, because the deckies from there are generally tolerable. There's really only two exceptions to everybody g'ttin' along on board this here ship. One's Sparky. All radio operators are nuts, but this one happens to be a nut *and* an asshole! No one likes him! Hell, I don't think he likes hisself!

"The other is niggers! Can't abide niggers!" Looking straight at Greg Russell, he said, "Take that nigger right there, for instance. Ya send him to school, teach him some manners, and dress him up. But down underneath it all he's still a nigger!"

Greg immediately came back. "Listen, you Georgia cracker. You're just pissed cuz all the colored boys where you grew up were screwin' your momma!"

I was too stunned to say anything. I kept looking back and forth between Greg and Roy, wondering if he was really this crazy or if this was some kind of test.

Finally, I stammered, "I don't know about the radio operator, but I've already met Greg, and I think he's a pretty nice guy."

Again, there was total silence, and everyone in the salon was staring directly at me. Finally, after what seemed forever, Greg said, "I guess he's okay. Anyway, that's twice he didn't back down from you, Roy. That shows me something."

Dumbfounded, I looked around and sputtered, "What the hell is going on here? Is this some kind of fraternity joke or something?"

At that point, the mate stood up, walked over to me, clapped me on the shoulder, and said, "You got that right. None of these clowns have ever grown up. They think they're still back at school hazing the youngies. The first time those two pulled that routine, I thought I was going to have a riot on my hands. I didn't realize they knew each other from when they attended license upgrade school together and that it was all an act. Now drink your coffee, and then come up to my room. I want to go over a few things with you."

Shaking his head, he walked out.

Everyone else was grinning at me as they prepared to leave. I walked to the sideboard, poked a few breakfast rolls that were left over, and decided against it. I gulped the remains of the coffee, put the cup in the sink in the scullery, and headed for the mate's room. Halfway there I decided that I'd better hit the head and detoured to the pilot's cabin.

Chapter 4

ESTABLISHING POSITION

"Have a seat," the mate said. "One of these days, Roy and Greg are going to pull that stunt in front of the wrong people, and there'll be hell to pay. You handled yourself pretty well there, William. I think you'll fit in okay here. I'm putting you on the twelve-to-four sea watch. It's a toss-up between you and the other third mate since you're both green, but the captain is the nervous type and doesn't sleep well when he doesn't trust the mate on the midwatch. I think he'll feel better with you on that watch."

"Thanks, Mate. I appreciate your confidence in me."

"Let's just say that, all in all, I trust Mass grads better than any of the other school-ship boys to know when to call the captain for advice. Some of these other know-it-alls think it's a sign of weakness or immaturity to call the captain when they're faced with a crossing situation. The fact that they either don't call him or call him too late is only a sign of stupidity.

"Fact of the matter is, the captain has a kind of sixth sense and always seems to show up on the bridge or look out his porthole at the right time." Pointing his finger at me, he said, "You don't want to not call the captain whenever there is a crossing situation. He will bury you if you do."

A crossing situation occurs whenever two ships are approaching each other in such a manner that one will cross in front of the other before they pass by. It is axiomatic and is covered by the *Nautical Rules of the Road*, both international and inland waterways versions. There are times when the ships appear to be on a head-to-head course or only slightly crossing, and these situations require careful attention. The one rule that is absolutely inviolate is the General Prudential rule, which states, in effect, that no one has the right of way through someone else. Common sense and survival instinct prevail.

"Okay," he went on. "What have you learned so far?"

Thinking this was going to be another test, I hesitated a few seconds before answering.

"Well, other than the fact that so far nothing is what it seems to be at first, I think if I survive this trip and don't irritate the captain, I'll probably learn enough to have a decent career in front of me."

He just harrumphed and didn't reply.

Noticing the ship's drawings on his desk that he and the captain had been looking at, I pointed to them and asked, "What kind of repairs are they doing?"

Ignoring my outstretched hand, he replied, "Mostly hull work, blast and paint. They have a few replacements going on in the engine room too. The steering engine slips, and the evaporator hasn't worked right since the ship came out of the yard. They're practically rebuilding it."

My immediate thought was, what does he mean by steering engine slippage? I'd hate to lose steering in a close-quarters situation. That could be disastrous. The evaporator provides all freshwater for the ship, for drinking, showering, and for the boilers in the engine room. While I have had plenty of saltwater showers, drinking water is critical, and saltwater in the steam drums would quickly ruin them.

I pressed further, saying, "I heard the captain say something about coamings." Since coamings are, in essence, the walls of the hatches, my first thought was of seaworthiness. "Do we have leaky hatches?"

"No, no, nothing like that. Just a pet peeve of the captain's. Don't worry about it. I'll take care of it."

Changing subjects, the chief mate outlined the daily schedule.

"We'll be on day watches the whole time we're in the yard. We'll set sea watches the midnight before we sail. If we're going to be in port less than twenty-four hours, which is almost never, we'll maintain sea watches. Otherwise, we'll switch to port watches. If we're in a foreign port, then you'll have the midnight-to-0800 hours watch. If we're in a US port, we'll most likely have night mates available, so we'll all be on day work, and you get the nights off. That applies to weekends in a US port also.

"Sea watches are routine. Both docking and undocking are standard routine. I'll be on the bow with the bos'n. You'll be on the stern. Either the second or other third mate is on the bridge, depending on the time of docking. If you're on watch when we dock, the other third will relieve you on the bridge. You and the other third will take turns relieving the second for supper. Got it?"

"Yes, sir!"

"Good! Have you looked over the hatch cover controls yet?"

"Not yet."

"Go do that now. The hatches are all hydraulic and work pretty well, but the controls are worked in sequence. If you go out of sequence, you could tip a cover. If you have any problems with them, get ahold of Boats, and he'll square it away."

I spent the remainder of the morning familiarizing myself with the hatch cover system and locating, opening, and closing all of the manhole access ways to the holds. I learned early on while on the training ship that you don't take anyone's word for something. Test it yourself. Then you're sure.

At noon, I went back to the pilot's cabin and cleaned up. I hadn't brought any work gloves with me, and there was grease on a lot of the hatch cover controls and winch stations. In addition to that, the entire ship was covered in a fine grit from the hull sandblasting.

Heading into the officers' salon, I preceded the captain and held the door for him. He breezed through without a word, obviously expecting me to play doorman for him. I couldn't help thinking, "He thinks he's royalty!"

The mate motioned me to come and sit with him, and after collecting a bowl of soup, I sat opposite him. In a low undertone, he began, "I see you're learning already to kowtow to the captain."

I looked at him, and, in an equally suppressed but tight tone, demanded, "What do you mean?"

"Holding the door for him. He expects stuff like that, and it don't hurt you any."

"Well," I replied, "one of the few things I learned growing up was to always be polite to your elders, and holding doors open for older men and women is just good manners."

"That may be," he replied, "but here, it isn't a matter of good manners, and it isn't optional. Here, the captain expects you and everyone else to treat him that way."

I just nodded and turned to my soup. Except for the soup, lunch was a cold lunch with salad, cold cuts, and fruit pie and cake for dessert. We had a choice of milk, coffee, tea, water, or bug juice—Kool-Aid or a derivative—to drink, and because the Stewards Department was still missing people, it was set up as a buffet. The soup was vegetable soup and was really good, definitely not out of a can. The cook had made it from scratch.

The only other person there besides the captain, the mate, and me was Greg Russell. He was hunched over a technical manual and eating, totally self-absorbed and oblivious to the rest of us. I was to learn that he had an incredible ability to concentrate on an issue and mentally obliterate the world around him.

As I worked my way through lunch, I was surreptitiously looking at the captain. He was extremely finicky and didn't eat so much as pick at his food. When he was finished, he pulled out a cigarette, inserted it into his cigarette holder, and lit it, blowing smoke ostentatiously into the air, looking for all the world like a male version of a vamp from a silent movie. The instant that thought flashed through my mind, I inwardly gave myself a start, thinking, "Don't let it show on my face." Dumb reaction, but that's what he was already doing to me mentally.

When he finished his smoke, the captain removed the cigarette from his holder and daintily snuffed it out in the ashtray. He then rose and left the sa-lon, leaving his dishes at the table. The mate leaned over and said, "What do you think of his cigarette holder?"

I couldn't help but grin, "It reminds me of the Penguin in *Batman and Robin*."

He burst out laughing. "Yeah, that really fits."

Just then, the other third engineer came in. He looked around and came over and introduced himself.

"Hi. I'm Pat Fahey, the third engineer." He was short, about five foot six, with a dark, closely trimmed beard and a monstrous handlebar mustache like that of Jerry Colonna, Bob Hope's regular sidekick.

"Hi. William Connelly, third mate. I saw your license when I came aboard and thought it was a guy I went to school with."

"If you're a Mass guy, then that was my second cousin. Same name, same occupation. Small world! He's sailing tankers out on the West Coast. Anyway, welcome aboard. In case you haven't already met him, beware of the second engineer. He's certifiable!"

I laughed and said, "I've already had the pleasure."

Interrupting us, the mate said to me, "After lunch, go up to the bridge and check the charts. I want to make sure we have all of them for the South American and African ports. It's the second's job, but I want to get a head start in case we have to order any new ones."

"Any particular parts of South America and Africa, Mate?"

"All of the east coast of South America and south and east Africa, including Madagascar, and west Africa as far up as Freeport, Liberia."

"Is the bridge locked up?"

"Oh yeah, I forgot. Wait a minute. I'll get the key for you."

"By the way, Mate, who is the second mate? Is he a regular too?"

"Sam Grossman. He's been aboard for about a year and a half, and he's supposed to come back. But with him, you never know."

"Why? Doesn't he like it here?

"Oh, I guess he likes it well enough, but he's moved around a lot. This is probably the longest he's ever stayed with a ship."

He handed me the key, and I made my way to the bridge. As I entered through the aft door, directly in front of me were the steering wheel, gyro compass, and binnacle containing the magnetic compass. To the right was the radar. In front was a full-view series of square ports, with one of them containing a rain screen. A rain screen is a circular window that rotates on a central axis using centrifugal force to keep the rain off the screen. On the starboard side aft bulkhead was a chart table and a loran-C unit. Loran is an acronym for *long-range navigation*. It used continuously transmitted radio signals generated from twenty-four American stations as well as Canadian and Russian stations. By plotting the signals and seeing where the different frequencies intersected on a loran chart, you were able to pinpoint the ship's position. On the port side aft bulkhead was the smoke detector system, showing readouts from all areas of the ship. Out on each of the bridge wings was a compass repeater and pelorus, used for taking sightings of navigation landmarks and other vessels in proximity.

Once on the bridge, I scoped out the radar, helm, smoke detector system, bridge wing repeaters, rain screens, and finally, the chart table. I went into the chart room behind the bridge and found the chart roster. I wasn't sure they would have one because merchant ships aren't run like the navy, the system the Mass Maritime Academy training ship was modeled on. I was grateful because at least I had a base document to work with. When I opened the top drawer, I found it filled with the current charts for the Gulf and East Coast, but not in sequence. Perusing the rest of the drawers, it became obvious that if the state of the charts was any indication, the second mate was lazy and sloppy.

Starting with the smallest-scale general sailing chart of South America and working my way up to the largest-scale charts, I put them in order from north to south. Using the smallest-scale chart as reference, I determined what was missing. On most of the charts, the latest notice-to-mariner corrections had been done more than two years ago, and they would need updating. A notice to mariners is a publication put out by the US Coast Guard that gives you all the changes to charts since they were last published. It's a mariner's bible. On the approach chart to Belém, Brazil, there were no notice-to-mariner updates at all, and the chart was six years old. The same for the Recife, Brazil, charts. I was surprised at how outdated they were since the ship had originally been on the South American run when it came out of the builder's yard.

I followed the same process for all the African charts. All the charts were there except for the approach charts to East London and Port Elizabeth. But the charts for Madagascar and everything north of Walvis Bay on the west coast were original issue date of 1958 and didn't show any updates from notices to mariners. So they were suspect.

By the time I finished, it was just after 1600 hours. I put everything away, shut off the lights, locked up, and went to find the chief mate.

He was sitting in his room smoking a cigarette, surrounded by papers that turned out to be requisition forms.

"C'mon in," he said. "This fuckin' paperwork is driving me nuts. We can't get a gallon of paint without filling out a two-page requisition in triplicate."

Leaning back and stretching, he asked, "What did you find up there in Sam's world?"

"Mate, it's a mess!" I recapped the chart situation for him. "We're missing some entirely, and I'm suspect of the ones that have been updated. Given the overall condition of the chart room, I'd recommend a complete new set of charts for the entire region. If we don't get them, someone is going to be spending a lot of time on the notices to mariners."

Once again came a harrumph and a muttered "More damn requisitions." Peering up at me over his reading specs, he said, "You know it would be you and the other third mate doing all the notices updates, don't you?"

"I guessed that would be the case."

He just sat there for a minute and finally said, "Okay, here's the deal. I'll order a full set of charts, but you now have a new job. Every midwatch, you go through the entire chart room and see that it's squared away. That's a fair trade-off, don't you think?"

"Mate, whatever you say is fine with me. But can I ask a question?"

"Yeah, sure."

"If we're going to South America, why update the African charts?"

"This company has a habit of rotating the South American ships into and out of the African run. I want to be prepared."

"One more question?"

"Okay."

"If the captain is so tough on everyone, how can the second get away with running such a sloppy show?"

"You aren't the first to ask that question. For whatever reason, the captain doesn't even talk to Sam, much less yell at him. We've all speculated, but the truth is, no one knows why. Instead, the captain drops not-so-subtle hints to me about the sloppy way I'm running the Deck Department."

"Can't you do something about him?"

Leaning back, he slowly scratched his chin. "The problem is, Sam ignores me. He yesses me to death but still does whatever he wants. And when I told the captain I was going to fire Sam, the old man flipped out! He insisted that I find a way to handle Sam without resorting to firing him. Well, Mr. Connolly, I just found my solution. You! By the way, Sam's also pretty sloppy about winding the chronometers, so check them every Saturday and make sure they're wound."

"Aye, aye, Mate."

A chronometer is just a fancy name for a clock—but an accurate clock, because you can only determine the longitude of your ship's position if you have an accurate time line. We would get a "time tick" from the radio operator based on Greenwich mean time (GMT) and match that to the chronometer when we wound it.

The rest of the week passed uneventfully, with Greg and I continuing to share a cab. Other than at lunchtime, I rarely saw Greg since he was usually in the bowels of the engine room. We would talk about the events of the day on the ride back to the Seamen's Church Institute. He was easy to talk to and loved to talk engineering. Even though I was interested, a lot of it was over my head. The morning ride was always quiet since neither one of us liked to gab in the morning. Staring out the cab window was like looking through a viewing port in an aquarium. Leaning against the seat made it seem that you were stationary while everything outside seemed to be swimming past you, and there were a lot of strange-looking swimmers in the Battery and Brooklyn.

For the most part, my days were boring. There were no cargo activities, and the captain wouldn't let us light off the radar, so I couldn't practice and familiarize myself with it.

On Friday morning, the new charts showed up, along with Second Mate Sam Grossman. At six feet three inches tall, nearly completely bald, and sporting a huge beer belly, he was, in every respect, a slob. Wearing a uniform that sported remnants of his last ten meals, he brought the concept of BO to new heights, or rather, depths.

I was on the bridge when he walked in with an armload of charts and said, "Move, will ya?" He then dumped the charts onto the chart table. Without another word, he left and went down below.

When I went down for a coffee break, he was sitting at a corner table all by himself. It was clear that both he and everyone else liked it that way.

I walked up to the mate and quietly asked, "Is that Grossman?"

"The name fits, doesn't it?"

Truer words were never spoken.

Standing there, aware of the closeness of Grossman even though normal conversational tones were muted by the sound-absorbing ceiling and wall tiles, I quietly told the mate what had transpired on the bridge. He just harrumphed again. It was clear to me by now that "harrumph" was the chief mate's method of articulating what he couldn't articulate. Funny enough, it worked.

Following up, he said, "That's typical. At least he didn't shove you out of the way. He did that with the previous third mate and got himself a black eye in return. Strangely enough, he didn't even complain. It was the third mate who told me, because he was scared he'd be fired, and he wanted to get his story in first. We decided to just forget the whole thing, since there were no witnesses other than the two of them.

"'Course, the third is gone, and he"—he gestured with his thumb toward Grossman—"is still here."

I got my coffee and sat down with the mate, all the while furiously thinking how I would deal with this human blob. I was pretty sure that sarcasm, in the manner I used with the second engineer, wouldn't work. That required thinking, something Grossman didn't seem too capable of. No, he would require a more animalistic approach.

While I was mentally sparring with myself, the mate, who had been staring at me the whole time, interrupted, saying, "Don't bother. Whatever you're thinking, he isn't worth the effort. Remember, it's the other third mate that isn't here anymore."

"Damn! You're scary. Do you read minds a lot?"

"Only when I'm being a Good Samaritan, and believe me, that ain't often."

As we were leaving the salon, the mate asked, "Did you check the charts he brought?"

"Not yet."

"Do that right away, will ya? I need to know 'cause the old man will flip if we don't have all the charts we need, and the ship chandler charges more on the weekend to deliver." A ship chandler is a shopkeeper that specializes in the sale of nautical items. An old-fashioned word in an historic industry.

I nodded and headed for the bridge.

About an hour later, I found the mate in his room and told him everything was there and that a few of the charts would still have to be checked against the notices to mariners for any recent updates because they were a year old. He thanked me, told me we would be signing articles that afternoon at 1400 hours, and suggested I fill out the allotment forms if I wanted any of my pay sent home.

At 1400 hours, I walked into the salon to find the captain, the chief steward in his role as purser, and a coast guard ensign named Jablonski witnessing the signing on of the crew. Off in the far corner were the mate and first engineer with a ledger of some sort.

The crew totaled thirty-nine souls. The Deck Department consisted of the officers—captain, chief mate, second mate, two third mates (one of whom was called a junior third)—and unlicensed deck hands. They were bosun, maintenance man, six able-bodied seamen (AB), and three ordinary seamen (OS).

The Engine Department consisted of the officers—chief engineer, first assistant engineer, second assistant engineer, two third assistant engineers (like the third mate, they are often referred to as junior thirds)—and the unlicensed hands. They were three oilers, three fireman water tenders (FWT), and one wiper. The oilers and firemen stood regular watches like an AB and

OS. The wiper was a day worker like the bosun and deck maintenance man. Both the Deck Department and Engine Department had places for cadets, but there were none on board this trip.

In addition, there was the radio officer (Sparky) and the Stewards Department. The chief steward also performed the duties of the purser. Under him were the chief cook, baker, third cook, salon messman, salon pantryman, officers' bedroom steward (BR), steward utility (gopher for the chief steward), the crew messman, who served the unlicensed crew, and the galley utility, who did most of the menial jobs like peeling potatoes.

The ship could carry up to twelve passengers, but there weren't any passengers onboard so the additional passenger utility and BR weren't required.

Each crew member in turn stepped up to the table and handed over his Z-card to the ensign, who looked at it and handed it to the purser. A Z-card is a merchant mariner's standard ID card, issued by the US Coast Guard. The purser did this little moue with his lips and asked the man if he wanted any allotments sent. If he did, the purser handed him some forms. After each man signed the articles, he filled out the forms, signed them and returned them to the purser, who gave him a copy. It was all pretty routine, but although I'd never done it before, I was very much aware that I was signing a contract with the steamship company. In reality, I was ceding control of a good part of my life to the captain.

It was a sobering thought.

Through all this, the captain was sitting back with one arm draped over the backrest, legs crossed, and smoking a cigarette, regally surveying his realm. He never spoke, and when one of the crew acknowledged his presence, he simply nodded.

When the crew finished at the captain's table, they went over to where the mate and first engineer sat. I learned that they were checking the men's union cards. It turned out both the mate and the first engineer were responsible for the maintenance and overtime of their respective departments, and they each kept a separate log for that purpose.

During a lull when there was no crew waiting in line, the mate said, "Go sign up." I immediately went over, said good afternoon to the captain, who graced me with a nod, and signed the articles. As I was reaching for the allotment forms from the purser, the captain stood up, reached out a hand, and said, "Welcome aboard, Mr. Connolly."

Stunned by his sudden cordiality, I managed to stammer, "Thank you, Captain," as I shook his hand. He then sat down and resumed his pose, once again behaving as if I didn't exist.

I went to a side table to fill out the allotment forms. If unmarried, we were allowed to name only a blood relative as recipient, usually mother or sister, so I named my ma. I signed the forms and returned them to the purser. I hadn't decided yet if he was queer, but he was definitely a sissy. His handshake was like holding a piece of wet, warm bread dough. I didn't like touching the guy. Despite that, I decided that I should make an effort not to be biased against the guy. It would be good diplomacy training for me, something I definitely lacked. Besides, from watching him, I could see he was very good at his job. Since that was the only thing we all owed to each other on the ship—doing our respective jobs right—it really was the only thing I or anyone else had any right to judge him by. As all this meandered through my head, I began to realize how difficult it was going to be to overcome my natural tendency to be highly opinionated on just about everything.

I went out on deck and walked to the forecastle. Usually referred to as foc's'le, it's the most forward part of the ship, used to store supplies and sometimes house the anchor windlass machinery and chain locker. A sailing ship term, it originally was the upper deck, forward of the foremast, and was the sailors' living quarters. That's where the term *before the mast* was derived.

It was warm and hinted at rain. I guessed it would get foggy later that evening. Lighting up a cigarette, I mused about the little ritual the captain had performed. Whether he only did it for new mates or for every mate signing on, it was well rehearsed and masterful. Yeah, that's the word: Masterful with a capital *M*.

Still and all, I was excited. Sunday, we'd be shifting over to the Twenty-Third Street pier in Brooklyn and start loading Monday morning. I would finally be doing what I had dreamed about for fifteen years, the last three of which had been very tough. Life was starting to get good!

Saturday was a blur. Fire and boat drills. I finally got to play with the radar. Checking every hatch cover again to ensure they opened and closed properly. Testing all the winches and capstans, and finally, at my insistence, getting a tour of the engine room from Greg. The mate thought I was nuts. Why in hell would a deckie want a tour of the engine room?

My old man had been an engineer. He sailed tankers during World War II and was on the Murmansk run. He had nothing but bad memories of that time, and he tried very hard to change my mind about going to sea. When I was twelve and not working on my many odd jobs, I used to help him repack the steam pumps at the distillery where he worked in Southie. I loved doing it. I still had the fascination for things that whirr and click and gurgle. The mate didn't understand that I became a deckie by default. I started out as an engineer but couldn't take the 135-degree heat in the engine room on the training ship, *Bay State*.

All the while I was running around, the ship was being floated. By the time I came out of the engine room, they had cleared all of the hull props, the wood and metal braces that kept the ship upright and balanced on its keel when not afloat. We were held in place by the mooring lines only.

By 0600 hours the next morning, I was impatiently sitting in the salon having a cigarette and drinking coffee. At 0700 hours, the mate arrived, grabbed a coffee, and sat down beside me.

"We'll be shifting around 1000 hours this morning. Don't panic back aft, you understand? This is pretty simple stuff as long as you pay attention and don't try and rush things. The docking pilot runs the show, and the captain just watches. The only difference is, since the other third mate hasn't shown up yet, the captain will be on the radio relaying orders. He doesn't trust Grossman enough to let him do it.

"When he tells you to single up, let the breast lines go first, then one of the spring lines, then the stern lines, until you're down to just one stern and one spring line. Because we're backing out of the dock, when he tells you to let go all lines, let the spring go last. It'll trail and can't get fouled in the prop. Make sure when the last stern line is let go, you haul it all the way in quickly, because the prop will suck it right in if you don't. Ya got all that?"

"I got it."

"Good."

"When we reach the berth at Twenty-Third Street, have Sturm handle the heaving line. He's the young German kid who's the AB on your watch. He's got an arm like Sandy Koufax."

"Yeah, I've talked to him a couple of times already. He's pretty intense."

"That he is, but he's German and knows how to obey orders and think at the same time. That's something you learn to appreciate in an unlicensed nowadays."

"Is there any particular sequence for tying up?"

"No, we'll play it by ear. Just make sure there's not too much slack in the lines so they don't get sucked into the prop."

"Thanks. I appreciate the heads up."

"Harummph!" he grunted. "Don't fuck up. I don't want to listen to the old man for the next month bitching about how inept these young kids are nowadays."

By 0930 hours, I was aft along with Sturm and Pickerel, the ABs, and Goode, the ordinary seaman on my watch. During the night, the shipyard crew had released all the port-side lines and snugged up the ship to the starboard side of the dry dock. I also noticed that they had taken in the breast line as well, so that was one less line to handle.

The tug came up about fifteen minutes later, and we took his towline and secured it on the port quarter bitt.

Chapter 5

GETTING UNDER WAY

At exactly 1000 hours, the captain called on the radio. "Mr. Connolly, single up."

I replied, "Aye, aye, Captain," and told the ABs to single up.

They threw the turns off the bitt for the second spring line and immediately wrapped a turn around the capstan. After I saw the line handlers free the line from the bollard, I told Sturm to haul away, and the line ran in smoothly, with Sturm running the capstan and Pickerel and Goode faking down the line as it came in. A capstan is a winch with the barrel of the drum in a vertical rather than horizontal axis. We repeated the maneuver with the stern lines.

At 1010 hours, the captain ordered, "Let go all lines aft."

We dropped the single spring and stern line and got them aboard without incident. While we were doing that, the tug had taken a strain on the towline, and slowly the ship began to drift astern out into the turning basin. There was nothing for me to do but watch at this point.

It wasn't until we were halfway clear of the dock that I could feel the rumble under my feet as the prop went slow astern.

When the bow cleared the dry-dock gate, the tug on the stern began to back down hard and to port, pulling the stern around in a wide arc. At the same time, the other tug that had been standing by until we cleared the dry dock swung in close to the bow and began pushing on the port side while securing another towline up forward. When we had spun about 120 degrees, the after tug stopped pulling and just lay at the end of the line. The forward tug stopped pushing, swung around to port, and proceeded to lead us out of the basin, with the after tug following like a dog on a leash.

All the while, I could feel and hear the change in direction and speed of the prop, and by looking over the side, I could pretty well gauge how much rudder was being applied. I found it fascinating but tried to maintain an aloof composure so as not to look like the green, young mate that I was.

Halfway over, the captain called and said to shift the tug line over to the starboard bitt because we would be docking port side to the pier.

It took about an hour to get over to Twenty-Third Street, where we spun the ship and backed into the north berth.

About two-thirds of the way in, the captain ordered, "Land the after spring line."

Without me saying anything, Sturm, who had heard the order, stepped to the rail and threw the heaving line to the line handlers on the dock. The mate was right about Sturm's throwing ability. He was a lefty like Koufax. It was a perfect throw, sailing just high enough over their heads so they could easily grab it without being close enough so they had to duck. He then wrapped the heaving line onto the eye of the spring line and flipped it over the rail it had been resting on. When the line handlers had it on the bollard, he threw a turn and a half on the bitt and waited for the next order. Pickerel retrieved the heaving line.

"Take a strain," came over the radio, and Sturm immediately stopped paying out on the spring and checked it, using the spring line as a brake for the ship, slowing it and pulling it alongside at the same time. I told Pickerel to take over from Sturm. Sturm fed a stern line through the port quarter chock and flipped the eye up over the rail. He then tied the heaving line to it. When the order came to put a stern line ashore, he threw another perfect strike to the line handlers and repeated the whole process. This time, after feeding it through the bitt, he led it to the capstan and took a turn on the drum.

Once again came, "Take a strain." This time, Goode ran the capstan while Sturm tended the stern line.

While we had been putting out the stern line, the after tug had slacked off on its towline, eased up alongside the starboard quarter, and began nuzzling the ship into the berth.

"Secure the stern line and land two more," came from the bridge.

With Goode keeping pressure on the line to keep it snug, Sturm tied off the stopper on the bitt, signaled Goode to ease off, and then threw two quick turns over the bitt. He then released the stopper. Stepping quickly to the other stern line, he fed it through the starboard quarter chock and flipped it over the rail. He then did the same thing for the third stern line. Picking up the heaving line, he threw strike three to the line handlers. This time, he wrapped both stern lines, and they hauled them both ashore to a bollard farther aft. I watched and made sure they dipped the second one before I gave the order to take a strain. Dipping a line is where the eye of one is passed through the eye of the other when placed on a bitt so that either one can be let go in any sequence. Not dipping is a sure sign of a rookie.

After securing all three lines, I called up to the bridge and reported in. The captain responded, "Very well. Tighten and secure the spring line and put out a breast line."

This time, Pickerel tied off the stopper on the spring line. When it was secure, Sturm unwrapped one of the turns from the bitt, led it to the capstan, and took a strain while Pickerel released the stopper. When I called to them that it was tight enough, Pickerel tied off the stopper. Sturm backed off the capstan, flipped the turns off the capstan, and took two turns on the bitt. Pickerel then released the stopper.

We then landed and secured the breast line.

I reported that all was secure aft, and this time the mate's voice came on and said, "Mr. Connolly, take your men and break out the gangway."

"Aye, aye, Mate," I replied and then turned toward Sturm with a look that said, "What now?"

To his credit, he didn't even smirk. He just started walking forward, and I followed him, with Pickerel and Goode trailing me.

"Release the binders," Sturm called to Pickerel.

They each took one end of the gangway and released the short wire and turnbuckle holding it in place.

Sturm then said, "Mr. Connolly, would you tend the winch while we push it out?"

I stepped over to the winch control and, at Sturm's command, backed off the bridle so that the gangway started to wobble. In a display of agility, Sturm swung one leg over the rail and kicked the top of the gangway, pushing it past the point of equilibrium. It slowly settled until the top end had pivoted ninety degrees and come to rest against the side of the ship, and both legs of the bridle bore equal weight on the bottom end. I continued to lower it until it reached a point about a foot over the cap log on the pier.

A cap log is a barrier, sometimes wood and sometimes concrete, standing about eight to twelve inches high, at the water side of the pier. It is intended to keep things, including people, from going off the edge of the pier.

Sturm stepped onto the pivot table and started to place the rail stanchions into their sockets, pinning them with a clevis pin.

He and Pickerel worked their way down the length of the gangway. After the last stanchion was in place, they threaded the safety line through the eyes in the stanchions. When everything was in place and tightened, all three of them stepped down to the pier and took hold of the gangway. They pulled it toward them to clear the cap log while I lowered it the rest of the way to the pier.

As they came over the top of the gangway, I called out, "Sturm, where's the safety net?"

"The bos'n's got a new one in the locker."

"Go get it, please."

When he came back five minutes later, he nodded at Pickerel, and without saying a word, they strung the net under the gangway and then returned aboard.

"We're done here, guys. You should report to the bos'n. Thanks for your help. You did a good job."

They both laughed, and I asked them what was so funny.

Sturm said, "Mr. Connolly, we were just doing our job, but you're the first mate I've ever sailed with that said thanks!"

With that, I smiled and said, "Well, maybe the other mates didn't need as much help as I did." They smiled again and walked off.

I wasn't sure whether I had just earned a little of their respect or had become the butt of a big joke to them. But I figured, what the hell; there was nothing lost by being civil and polite, because they knew I was as green as grass anyway.

I went looking for the mate.

Chapter 6

CARGO WATCH

It was 0700 hours Monday. I was standing out on the main deck forward of the house, leaning on the railing, waiting for the longshoremen to arrive. It was already eighty degrees and muggy. Rain wasn't forecast, but lots of scud cumulus made it feel and look like the prelude to a gale. Earlier, the mate had told me there were four gangs ordered for an 0800 hours start. We were going to be loading in numbers two, three, and five lower holds, and number four lower tween deck.

When longshoremen are hired to load or discharge cargo, they are always hired in "gangs." Depending on the type of cargo to be loaded, there are anywhere from eighteen to twenty men in a gang. A gang is led by a foreman, usually called gang boss, although that title varies from port to port. There are two winch or crane operators to run the equipment that hoists the cargo; a signalman to direct the winch operators in areas where they don't have direct line of sight; eight to ten holdmen who physically handle the cargo in the hold of the ship and operate forklifts when needed, one of whom also acts as a signalman; two dock landers who guide the draft of cargo as it's being landed on the dock and then unhook the ropes/wires; and at least two forklift drivers for the pier to move the cargo away from the cargo hook and bring it to its final point of rest on the pier. Associated with each gang is at least one checker, responsible for the clerical tallying of the cargo being loaded and/or discharged.

From Maine to Texas in the United States, all of the longshoremen/checkers are members of the International Longshoremen's Association (ILA).

I had been sitting with the mate when the stevedore superintendent, Bill DiBlasi, came in to go over the stow plan. After Bill had left, I asked, "Don't they check the gear certificate anymore?"

"Anyplace else they will. Here, they don't have to. Only MorMac ships dock here. The office has a copy of every certificate for every ship, so they know what's current and what isn't. When he asked me if everything was okay, he was really asking if anything was wrong with the gear that they might not know about. Since I said everything was fine, he was satisfied. Remember, these are our people here. This is our house stevedore.

"We won't be full when we sail from Jacksonville. We're still out of sync with the normal schedule of ships because of coming off the 'Nam run. Number five lower hold has Lutheran Aid cargo. That's mostly baled clothes, crated pots and pans, plastic dishes, a lot of odds and ends. It's hard to hurt that stuff, so just make sure they stow it tight. I don't want to spend a fortune on securing. We got army six-bys in number three and number four lower holds," he said, referring to the two-and-a-half-ton, double-rear-axle cargo trucks built especially for the army, mainly by General Motors. "It's AID or lend-lease cargo. I want them all fore and aft, nothing on the burthen. Space isn't a problem, and I don't want to be chasing a six-by around at sea. Also, make sure they disconnect and tape the battery leads. Things move at sea, and we can't afford any sparks from bare leads that touch something. You are to personally check every one of them. Understand?"

"Yessir, Mate."

"We got some canned goods and radios, TVs and such, and I decided to put them into the refrigerated lockers in the upper tween deck. They're the only cargo spaces that we can close the doors on and lock."

"None of it's reefer cargo, is it?"

"No. The refrigeration system will be off. The longshoremen here don't bother taking that stuff, at least while we're loading it. I guess they get their mitts into it before it ever gets to the ship. It costs us a little more to handle it here into the locker, but once it's in there, it's safe. It's less likely to take a walk at any of the South American ports because they can't get into the reefer lockers.

"Number two will be all household effects. Watch out for leakers. The moving companies pack these things, and they generally do a good job, but every once in a while, they'll stick something in there that shouldn't be there, like a gasoline can or paint. It makes a mess, and it's dangerous goods, so we have to watch it."

Standing at the after, offshore corner of number three hatch, I watched the winch operator as he smoothly slid the cargo falls back and forth between the pier and the hold. He was moving along at a good pace, but there wasn't any of the herky-jerky motion that I had witnessed so often back in Boston as a kid. The draft of cargo lifted cleanly off the ground and transitioned from vertical to horizontal in a perfect arc, clearing the inboard rail by no more than four feet, but never less than three feet. From there, he took it over the coaming and settled it down into the hold swiftly but gently. He had a real good touch for the winch controls. He looked at the signalman on deck and the holdman giving hand signals, although I could tell he really wasn't paying attention to them. He always maintained a fluidness that didn't match their often frantic waving of hands. Having tried my hand at running winches in the past, I was impressed by how good he was.

We loaded half a dozen POVs (privately owned vehicles), all used, into the upper tween deck of number three hatch. The mate had the wood butchers (waterfront vernacular for carpenters employed to secure cargo) use Spanish windlasses to secure them instead of the more costly wires and turnbuckles that we used on heavier trucks. The Spanish windlass was just some half-inch sisal rope looped two or three times around a part of the car frame and a lashing point, usually a D ring on the deck, and the ends of the rope were tied together. A two-foot-long wooden stick was then placed between the strands of rope and wound like an elastic band until the rope was tight. When it was tight enough, the wooden stake was pushed through the rope so that one end of it rested against the deck or other structure so that it couldn't unwind and get loose. During the voyage, the mate had to check them every day, because the rope would initially stretch quite a bit and loosen up. You definitely don't want cars thrashing around in the tween deck while at sea.

Chapter 7

SEA WATCH

It was our third day of loading, and it was hectic all day with the final loading and securing of the cargo and the taking on of stores. A small gang of longshoremen was hired six to bring the stores aboard. This was all supplies for the ship's crew but ran the gamut from food to acetylene gas bottles to five-gallon buckets of paint.

The mate was in a foul mood. The captain was ragging on him all day long about nitpicking crap, and was proving the theory of "shit flows downhill." Tony Adams and I did our damnedest to avoid him all day.

The sailing board was posted for 2100 hours, and we had set sea watches at 0800 hours, but the mate still had us both out watching the cargo operations. The actual loading finished around 1500 hours, but the wood butchers were still aboard and weren't expected to finish until 1900 hours.

Tony Adams was the other third mate. He came aboard yesterday afternoon just as the mate was beginning to piss and moan about the possibility of having to stand a watch at sea if we sailed shorthanded. That was occurring more regularly in the past year. When I graduated, most of my class got commissioned as ensigns in the navy reserve, but we were discouraged from going into active duty because the need for deck and engine officers in the merchant marine was so great at the time. Our alternative to active duty was to sail in the merchant marine for eight months out of twelve for three consecutive years. This was a blessing that many of us would come to realize as the war in Vietnam dragged on and we lost friends and relatives.

Tony was a Fort Schuyler grad, and we hit it off right from the start. Fort Schuyler, located in the Bronx, was a division of the State University of New York. It was one of the four state maritime colleges, along with Massachusetts Maritime Academy, Maine Maritime Academy, and Texas Maritime Academy. There is also the US Merchant Marine Academy located at King's Point, New York. They all specialize in training merchant marine officers. Tony and I had something in common. This was the first trip for both of us, and we were both terrified of the captain. Fear can be both motivational and a cause for bonding. We also both suffered from the same affliction. We whistled unconsciously as we worked. Not only was this irritating to those around us, but it set the superstitious guys on edge. It's supposed to be bad luck to whistle on board a ship. I've heard a number of reasons why, but the best explanation came from my seamanship instructor, a venerable "old salt." It hails from the days of sailing ships. Whistling was thought to bring on gales and other storms. There was a practical reason as well. Since bosuns' whistles (commonly known as fifes) were used to relay orders, any unauthorized whistling could be mistaken and result in blocks and sheets being let go improperly. There could be dire consequences. His best reason he saved for last. "Whistle in front of me, and I'll shove a fid up your ass to help you remember not to."

In any case, we both made a conscious effort to not whistle because it seemed to offend just about everyone on board, but we weren't always successful in our efforts.

Tony and I decided that we would work in opposite directions, moving fore and aft on the offshore side, with one of us staying on deck at all times. It's standard safety practice to stay on the offshore side as much as possible to avoid having to dodge the cargo falls swinging back and forth.

All but one gang at number three hatch had finished. An old guy stood on deck at the inshore rail acting as a signalman for the winch operator. He wasn't doing anything strenuous, but I noticed he seemed to be wheezing and having a hard time breathing. I crossed inshore aft of the hatch so I was behind him at the railing. Just as I reached him, he gasped and clutched his chest, sagging against the rail and falling to the deck. Having just finished first aid training, I immediately realized that he was having a heart attack. Running aft, I yelled to the gangway watch to call for an ambulance, ran into the house up to the purser's room, and pounded on the door. When he opened it, I shouted, "Where's the oxygen bottle? Someone's having a heart attack!"

He just stood there with his jaw slack. I looked around and noticed the oxygen bottle was on a rack by his desk in the corner. Grabbing it, I ran back down to the deck, straightened the guy out, and affixed the mask attached to the oxygen bottle to his face. He wasn't completely out cold, but he wasn't lucid either, kind of mumbling and incoherent. I tried to listen to his heartbeat, but the background noise drowned out the sound. I felt for a pulse and got one, although it seemed to be pretty weak. By this time, the longshoremen had all stopped and gathered around. I overheard one of them say, "Rocco don't look too good. Has anyone got ahold of Frankie yet?"

I told the nearest guy to go check with the gangway watchman and make sure he had called for an ambulance. I then went back to talking to the old guy, supporting his head and neck and telling him everything was going to be okay, that the ambulance was on its way. I wasn't sure if anything I said was registering with him, but I remembered as part of my training to keep them awake and keep talking to them for reassurance and also to serve as a distraction.

After what seemed to me to be an hour but was really only ten minutes, a fire engine and ambulance pulled up to the foot of the gangway. In no time, they had him on a stretcher and on the way to the hospital.

Later, after everything returned to normal and the gang had finished at number three hatch, Tony and I stood at the hatch looking over the coaming into the forward end. It was open all the way down to the lower hold because the wood butchers were just finishing up the securing. Some of them were climbing up through the manholes, and the leader was lowering a rope to the remaining guys in the hold so they could lift out their saws and wrenches and the extra wire, clips, and turnbuckles they hadn't used. It took them about twenty minutes. As the last man was coming up, I went up on the control platform to shut the hatches. Just as I reached the platform, I heard Tony shout, "Hey! What the hell are you doing?"

Looking over the railing, I saw him flying across the top of the aft section of the hatch cover and jumping off the cover onto the deck directly in front of one of the biggest human beings I had ever seen. The guy was standing there, stock still, glaring at Tony.

"How'd ya like it if I went and set your house on fire? Well, this ship is my house, and you were about to set it on fire!"

It was then that I noticed the guy was holding a lit cigarette in his hand.

Just then, the ship boss came up to Tony. I couldn't hear what he said, but it sure had an effect on the big guy. He bent over, put the butt on the deck, and ground it out with his shoe. He said something to Tony and hurried off the ship. The ship boss looked at Tony, smiled, patted him on the shoulder, shook his hand, and left the ship.

I called to Tony, "Is everyone out from below?"

"All clear!"

I covered the lower tween, then the upper tween, and finally the main hatch cover. I shut off the stop valves to the controls and closed the control panel door.

Landing on deck, I asked Tony, "What happened?"

"The big guy was about to flip his butt into the hold, and that's when I yelled at him. It turned out okay, but man, if I hadn't instinctively reacted and had time to actually look at that guy, I don't think I would have said anything. I'd have gone down the hold and found the butt myself. He must have lit it when he was in the hold, because he just came up on deck. Did you see how big he was? Holy shit! If he had ever hit me, I'd probably be dead!"

We turned and walked aft, running into Boats as we reached the house.

"Boats, number three is shut tight. You can have the men dog it down now."

"Aye, aye, Mr. Connolly. They're working their way forward."

As Tony moved away, in a lower tone, I said, "Say, Boats, is there anything else I'm supposed to check with you about before we get called out for sailing?"

"Nope. You're doin' just fine." He then grinned at me as he walked forward.

I followed Tony into the house, and we went to our respective rooms to clean up.

When I entered the salon, the captain was holding court, regaling Tony Adams about the absolute power a captain had while at sea, a god in his own world. Even though he was addressing Tony, no one else in the room was speaking. It was a little eerie, but then I remembered the mate telling me the captain expected to be treated like royalty. Nobody talks when the king is talking!

The captain was relating this to Tony as if he was telling him a private joke, but Tony's reaction mirrored the way I felt. You could read on his face what he was thinking:

Please, God, don't let the captain get pissed at me!

The captain finished his story, and then, fixing Tony with a piercing glare, he pointed his finger at me and said, "Mr. Connolly, what is the moral of my little fable?"

Caught completely by surprise, I hesitated a few seconds. When nothing intelligible emerged from my lips, the captain turned to Tony and raised an eyebrow, implying that he was to answer the question.

"I guess it means I should do everything the right way, and then I won't incur the wrath of God."

The captain had the good grace to laugh and say, "That's almost right."

Looking at me he said, "Would you like to try again?"

"It means I should do everything the captain's way, Captain."

With a smirk, he said, "That's better yet."

Turning to the mate he said, "Mr. Mate, we might have a couple of decent prospects here after all."

With that, he made another of his royal exits, and there was an audible rush of air into the vacuum his departure had created.

Everybody started talking at once. Roy Oliver came over to me and Tony, slapped us both on the back, and said, "Y'all better just quit while you're ahead cuz that's the nicest thing I ever heard him say about a third mate, and I doubt he'll ever be that nice to y'all again. Y'all better go change your undies, too, cuz you both looked like you were gonna shit yourselves!"

He wasn't too far from the truth. He then broke out in that braying laugh of his and walked out.

As the mate got up to leave, he said, "Be on your stations at 2000 hours."

Chapter 8

THE FIRST TEST

At 2000 hours, I was aft with ABs Sturm and Pickerel and my ordinary, Goode. The undocking went without any glitches. Because we were only going to Baltimore, just a short run, and there wasn't any bad weather predicted, the mate instructed me to leave the mooring lines on deck instead of stowing them away. Sturm showed me that, despite all of the training on the *Bay State*, there were stills things to be learned from on the job. He "suggested" that we should pass the bight through the eye on one end of each mooring line and loop it over the bitt so, if the line should be washed overboard, it would be belayed at one end and we could retrieve it. I followed his advice, although I suspect he would have done it anyway whether I had agreed with him or not.

After we cleared the berth and were in the channel, the tug came alongside. The docking master went over the rail onto the tug, and it pulled away, leaving the pilot to finish the short trip to the pilot station. Although I knew I should get some sleep because I had the midwatch, I was too excited about being on the first leg of an actual non- training-ship trip to sleep. I went up to the flying bridge, being careful to avoid being seen by the captain, and stayed there until we neared Ambrose light and the pilot boat came alongside to disembark the pilot. As we turned south, the lights from New York started to fade. Knowing there would be distant shore lights to starboard and nothing but ocean to port to look at, I went to my room, lay on the bunk, and dozed off.

At 2330 hours, the ordinary from the eight-to-twelve watch knocked on my door and woke me up for my watch. Already dressed, I just splashed some water on my face, took a leak, and went down to the salon to check out the midnight meal. The salon was dim, with only one light over the serving counter. There was an aroma reminiscent of a combination of the stew and apple pie we had for supper. The steward had left a tray of cold cuts, bread and rolls, pickles and olives, and some pound cake. I soon learned that the second cook, who did all the baking, had a fixation for pound cake. Although it was pretty good, it became easy to pass up after two weeks. I munched a piece of cake and washed it down with a cup of coffee. Pouring a second cup, I went up to relieve Tony.

The custom is to relieve the watch ten minutes before the hour to have time to find out the position and what, if anything, is happening. In the commercial world, it's also considered a courtesy. I had scrupulously adhered to this practice when on the training ship because, in addition to it being a courtesy, if you didn't do it, you got your balls busted by your classmates and got written up for demerits. Demerits equaled lost liberty, something no one wanted. At the end of a watch, you get antsy, especially if it's at sea and there's nothing going on. The last half hour always seems like forever, and you tend to get testy if your relief isn't there on time.

I walked onto the bridge. "Hi, Tony. What's going on?"

"Not much. We're on course one hundred eighty-five degrees doing nineteen knots. Visibility is good, and we've got four ships in sight and a couple of small craft. Three of the ships are passing us to port heading north, and the fourth is trailing us and losing ground. We're doing about three knots faster than her. All the small craft are inshore of us and at least three miles off. None of them are crossing or even approaching."

Scanning the radar, I quickly confirmed the positions, speed, and bearings of the four ships and noted that in addition to about six small craft, there was a lot of clutter on the screen farther in toward shore, about a half mile offshore.

"What's causing the clutter?"

"No idea. The captain was up here a little after 2300 hours. He said it could be anything, and, so long as the range didn't change and it was consistent, not to worry about it."

"Well, if he isn't worried, then I won't be. Anything else I need to know?"

"No. The course is laid out on the chart. Oh yeah, if you get any crossing situations, call the captain right away. Other than that, you got it."

"Okay. You're relieved. Good night."

As I was saying this, Sturm, my AB, was relieving the helmsman. He called out the heading and stated that the helmsman was relieved.

I walked out on the port wing. It had cooled some since we'd left port, with light cloud cover and a slight southeast wind. I took bearings on all the ships at a five-minute interval, and the bearing was changing appropriately. Then I went to the starboard wing, checked the ship following us, and scanned the horizon for lights. I could make out the lights of some small craft, and there were some distinguishable shore lights. Going back in, I asked Sturm who was on lookout.

"Brian Goode."

It occurred to me that I hadn't heard any bells struck at midnight. I was about to say something to Sturm when I remembered that bells were a military tradition, and I was now in a commercial world. The only bell I would be hearing would be a signal from the lookout if he saw anything.

I called the lookout on the 1MC, the onboard communication system, just to check it out, and it worked fine.

Stepping back out on the port wing, I lit a cigarette and thought, "This is it. This is what I sweated for. Incredible!" The cigarette burned down, and I was about to flip it overboard but caught myself. With just a light southeast breeze, the wind was mainly caused by the speed of the ship, and there was a good chance the cigarette would blow back on deck. Opting instead to grind it out on the heel of my shoe, I tossed it in the wastebasket inside the chart room.

Just as I was turning to look at the chart, the 1MC buzzed. The lookout reported that he saw a light about one point on the starboard bow. Scanning the radar, I saw there was a blip about nine miles out. Deciding to use visual rather than radar, I walked out to the repeater compass on the starboard wing. Aligning the pelorus, a ring that sits on the compass repeater with uprights for aligning targets, I took a bearing. It read 188 degrees. Using the glasses, I could make out a masthead and range and an intermittent flicker of a starboard running light. After five minutes, the bearing read 191 degrees. Considering that we closed to within seven miles and the bearing only opened three degrees, it was going to be a pretty close passing. For about five seconds, I wavered about gutting it out, but caution won, and I called the captain.

He picked up almost before the phone stopped ringing, and I reported the situation to him. He hung up without saying anything. A minute later, he walked onto the bridge, looked at the radar, and asked, "Any traffic to port?"

"No, Captain. All the prior traffic has already passed, and we're clear to port."

He walked out to the starboard wing, peered at the oncoming ship for a few seconds, walked back in, and headed for the door to the companionway. As he passed me, he said, "If there's any change, call me. Otherwise, keep it going."

"Aye, aye, Captain,"

Then he was gone. I relaxed but still stayed glued to the repeater until the ship was abeam. Then I went back into the bridge and lit my second cigarette.

At 0200 hours, the second AB, Charley Pickerel, relieved Sturm at the helm. While the ABs took two-hour stints at the helm, during their off time, they would relieve the ordinary at lookout for about fifteen minutes each hour. It was the ordinary's job to call the next watch, so his last half hour of watch was usually in the crew mess.

Around 0230 hours, the inshore clutter mysteriously disappeared, and a few small boats were distinguishable, but well inshore and out of harm's way. Beyond that, there was no activity.

At 0350 hours, the AB for the four-to-eight watch came onto the bridge and relieved Charley. I asked the AB if he had seen the second mate. He said no, so I told Charley to check on the second on his way down. Five minutes later, Charley came back and said that the second had been sound asleep, and he had just rousted him. I thanked him and told him to hit the sack.

Finally, at 0410 hours, the second arrived on the bridge and immediately started telling me off on how *my* ordinary hadn't woke him up on time.

"I'll tell you what," I said. "I'll ream his ass when he comes on watch at noon. I'll also tell him to double-check five minutes after he wakes you the first time, and if he can't wake you the second time to pour a cup of cold water on your head."

"Listen, you little snot nose," he snarled. "Just have your fuckin' ordinary do his job right and don't give me any of your shit!"

Rather than dig myself any deeper, I just said, "Sure."

"What's our course and position?"

I dutifully reported them, told him there was nothing in sight, and when he said, "You're relieved," I scurried off the bridge, seething inside but knowing I had pushed the envelope a little on our first encounter. As I passed the captain's stateroom, a voice called, "Sonny," and I froze in my tracks.

Approaching the door, I said, "Yes, Captain." He was out of sight in his bedroom and didn't come into the stateroom. It was eerie talking to a bodiless voice.

"I don't believe you made any friends just now, but chances are you'll get relieved on time in the future. Good night, sonny."

"Good night, Captain."

As I lay down in my bunk, my last waking thought was, "Learn to start your brain before you shoot your mouth off. Life will be a lot simpler."

Standing in his usual port corner of the bridge, the second sulked and thought, "Goddamn snotty young bastards. They all think they're better than me. Snotty school-ship assholes, all of them. Coming up through the hawsepipe the way I did is a lot harder than what they did. Even the friggin' mate bitched at me until the captain backed him off. The captain—there's another asshole

I can't stand either, the son of a bitch! Even though he's covered for me when I complained to him, I know he looks at me like I'm trash. He helped Ma out when Seymour died, and for whatever reason, he's helped me. I should be grateful, but he's such an arrogant shit that I just want to smack him."

With no one to take out his anger on, he turned to the AB and barked, "Watch your helm! You're wandering all over the place!"

The AB had known him long enough to just say, "Aye, Mate!" and not remind him that the ship was on autopilot.

Chapter 9

BALTIMORE

We picked up the Chesapeake Bay pilot at 1400 hours on Thursday and started up the bay. I spent eight days in dry dock in Baltimore while on the training ship, so I remembered the city. But since I had been in my engineering half of the training cruise, I never saw anything but gauges, indicator glasses, and deck plates, making the bay a new experience.

Although the pilot navigates the ship in these cases, officially he's only an advisor, and the captain is always in charge. Therefore, as the mate on watch, I plotted the course changes and verified all of them with actual bearings on landmarks and range markers. There were two differences between what I was doing and what the pilot was doing. First, he gave the helmsman the actual course change and steering orders; and second, he was doing it all by memory, while I scurried around like a gerbil doing it by scribbles on the chart.

We passed the Naval Academy off to port and proceeded up the bay, going under the Chesapeake Bay Bridge, passing Fort Carroll and Fort McHenry. The latter is a well-known landmark that inspired Francis Scott Key to write the words to our national anthem. Fort Carroll, its neighbor, is relatively unknown except to local history buffs. Named after Charles Carroll, an original signer of the Declaration of Independence, it is a tiny—under four acres—man-made island located in the middle of the harbor approach. Almost due south of the new Dundalk Marine Terminal being built on the site of the old Dundalk Harbor Airfield, it's approximately on an east-west line between Sparrows Point, home of the Bethlehem Shipyard, and the northernmost point of the entrance to Curtis Bay.

The idea to build it was conceived in 1818, but construction didn't start until 1849. The person who supervised the construction was none other than Robert E. Lee, who happened to be head of the Corps of Engineers at the time and resided in Baltimore. Fort Carroll seemed to be the "too little, too late" fort, in that it was inspired by the memory of the War of 1812 but was never a factor in the Civil War, World War I or World War II. It has served as a lighthouse—they moved it three times mainly due to deterioration of the structure—a temporary shelter for foreign seamen, a firing range, and a small-arms training area. In 1958 the Corps of Engineers sold the fort to a local Baltimore businessman named Benjamin Eisenberg. Apparently, he thought it would make a good site for a gambling casino, but to date, there is nothing but rotting structure, overgrowth, and birds there.

We finally docked at North Locust Point at 0100 hours.

Baltimore is a lot like Boston: the neighborhoods are very ethnic. Locust Point is heavily Polish, Irish, and German, and a lot of the white longshoremen lived there. The Negro longshoremen lived more on the west side of the city. You would occasionally get both Negro and white gangs working on the ship at the same time but in different hatches. They would never mix the gangs, and I never saw a white man in a black gang or vice versa. They all seemed to get along okay in a live-and-let-live fashion, but there didn't seem to be any real friendliness between them, only a sort of acceptance.

The longshoremen started work at 0700 Friday morning. That afternoon, the mate told me to leave the hatches open when the longshoremen finished for the day. I thought he was trying to avoid another argument with the ship boss.

When we first went to open the hatches, Tony and I climbed up and started our usual routine. I heard, "Hey, Mate, knock it off, or we knock off!"

It was the ship boss, the senior ILA guy. I had no idea what was bothering him, but having grown up on the Boston waterfront and understanding how temperamental the longshoremen can be, I stopped and asked him, "What's wrong?" It turned out that opening the hatches was a union job.

"Who do you have in your crew that knows our hatch system? We have the new hydraulic hatch covers."

"I don't have anyone."

"I don't want to step on anyone's toes, boss, but how are you going to get the hatches open if you don't have anyone that knows how to open them?"

"Wait a minute," he said, leaned over the rail, and called down to the dock.

After a couple of minutes, a tall, thin guy came over the top of the gangway and walked up to us.

"This is Weezer," the ship boss said. "You go open up the hatch with him and show him how to do it."

"Come on, Weezer," I said and proceeded to do just that. He immediately understood the danger of opening them out of sequence and having them topple. I guess he had enough common sense to figure that if anything happened, it was going to be him or his buddies that got hurt and not the mates.

Later, after explaining to the mate what happened, he told Tony and me to let the ILA guys open the hatch, but he wanted one of us right there with them.

We had broken sea watches, so I was free for the night. At sea we stand watches four hours on, eight hours off. In port it's changed if we are scheduled to get relief mates from the union hall. Then we work day work and have the nights off.

I'd seen downtown Baltimore before, and, not being in the mood to visit the Block, Baltimore's equivalent to Boston's Combat Zone—strip clubs and overpriced drinks—I decided to go to Hausner's and get a good meal. Over in Highlandtown, Hausner's was a well-known tourist attraction, interesting enough with decent food.

Tony had already left. A friend of his had picked him up and taken him home to one of the suburbs, a place called Westminster. I told Tony I'd cover for him the next day. I didn't mind, and I figured it was better if he owed me a few favors. The mate had blessed it, so he was gone for the night.

Leaving, I stopped at the mate's room.

"I'm heading for Hausner's. You want to come along? I'll treat."

"No, thanks. I'm watching the store. We couldn't get a night mate."

"If you have something you want to do, I'll take the watch," I said, hoping like hell he wouldn't take me up on the offer even though I felt obliged to make it.

"Nah, it's okay. There's nothing happening, and I'll take it easy tonight. Go out and enjoy yourself. By the way, what time you think you'll be back?"

"I don't know. I might stop for a drink after, but it won't be late."

"Take your time. You should have a little fun. You're still young enough to enjoy it."

I headed out, went down the gangway, walked past the head of the pier, crossed over the rail track, and walked up to Fort Avenue, where I caught a cab to Hausner's. Now that I was actually earning a paycheck, I figured I didn't have to keep such a firm grip on every nickel.

Over on Eastern Avenue heading toward Dundalk, Hausner's is really an interesting place. Everybody who has ever sailed into Baltimore knows about it. It's good food at reasonable prices. The waiters and waitresses are ancient, somewhat acerbic in their remarks to customers, but in a bantering rather than nasty manner. They call everyone "hon" whether they've known you for ten years or ten minutes. The walls of the place are filled with paintings of every description, a few of which might actually be worth something. Most of it, at least to my untutored eye, was junk, but interesting junk. I particularly liked the nudes hanging on the walls in the men's bar.

Around 2230 hours, I headed back after deciding that the two desserts I had would make up for the second drink I didn't have. The cabbie dropped me off at the head of the pier, and I walked down to the ship. As I topped the gangway, it occurred to me that no one was watching the gangway. With no night mate, the mate should have had the bosun assign a crew member to tend the gangway. About to step into the house and check out the crew mess, I glanced up and thought I saw a flash of light coming from number three hatch. As I walked forward, I heard voices, muted but audible. Instinctively, I crouched down, went back to the after end of the hatch, and crossed to the outboard side where the deck was darker. Peering over the corner of the coaming, I could see two figures standing alongside the inboard coaming on top of the cargo. They seemed to be leaning against the coaming.

Just then, the feeling hit me. This time, there was no preliminary anxiety. It went right into a full-tilt spell. I started shaking, went down to one knee, and leaned my head against the bulkhead. I was pouring sweat and getting nauseous, but the cold bulkhead acted like a buttress against the onslaught. The two figures leaning; I had lived this scene before, had been here before. Full-blown déjà vu, and it scared the shit out of me! I knew what was going on in the hold but slowly forced myself to look again in hopes that it would change. It didn't.

As my eyes adjusted and the shaking eased, I could see they were, indeed, leaning. Each held onto the end of a tarpaulin, using it like a tent over a section. At the same time, I realized that the flashes of light I had seen came from underneath the tarp.

I thought about finding the mate, but then another figure emerged from under one end of the tarp. It was the mate! Even in the bad light, there was no mistaking him.

He said something to the guy at his end, and they lowered the tarp. When they did, I noticed a fourth person setting something down that had a hose attached. Looking up, I saw a gaping hole in the side of the coaming about three feet square. All of a sudden, everything clicked. They had been using an oxyacetylene torch to cut a hole in the coaming. But why?

I could discern that the two men holding the tarp were the bosun and Roy, the second engineer. The guy doing the burning was Bill, the chief engineer. What the hell was going on?

I wanted to stand up and ask them, but instinct told me not to. Between the oddity of the situation and my bout with the déjà vu weirdness, the last thing I wanted to do was confront anyone. The feeling I get when the spell hits just saps me and makes me want to curl up and hide. Instead of approaching, I backed away, went all the way aft to behind the house, and climbed up to the flying bridge on the outside ladders. From there, lying down on the offshore corner, I could see clearly into the hatch. But they couldn't see me since there weren't any cargo lights on.

I waited and watched.

The chief had climbed into the hole in the coaming and started handing out what looked to be small boxes, about two feet long by two feet high and one foot wide. The others were relaying the boxes across the hatch to a ladder against the corner of the coaming where I had been. I hadn't seen the ladder from my vantage point because it was in the shadow below the top of the coaming. If I had stayed there, whoever came up that ladder would have stepped on me. Boats did the walking across the hatch, and Roy handed the boxes up the ladder to the mate, now on deck. The mate walked to the railing and dropped the boxes overboard. They must have been fairly heavy because they sank immediately, no bobbing around.

I counted roughly a hundred boxes that they dumped overboard. They then switched to smaller cartons that looked like cases of beer, but instead of dumping them all overboard, the mate would stack about every fourth or fifth one on the deck. He stacked about twenty of them. Roy climbed on deck with him, and they carried them forward into the bosun's locker.

The chief and Boats started to wrestle the piece of plating they had cut out back up into the hole, when Roy called softly, "Not yet. I gotta get something in there." Squirming back into the hatch, he disappeared into the opening. When he came out a few minutes later, he lugged what looked like a burlap sack.

"What the hell's that?" the mate whispered.

"Something personal I stashed. Nothing to do with the other stuff."

"Get moving," growled the mate.

While Boats held it, the chief placed a few tack welds on the plate to keep it in place. Boats then picked up the tarp, and, holding it in both hands above his head, leaned into the bulkhead and effectively covered the chief while he rewelded the plate. I could still see some light flash, but no one else would be able to unless they looked directly into the hatch. Before the chief was done, Roy and the mate returned and helped Boats with the tarp.

All this time, I wondered how they had avoided setting anything on fire. The cargo under them consisted of dry wooden crates and was highly flammable.

By this time, my clothes were soaked from the night dew on the deck when I first lay down. I sporadically shivered, but I didn't dare leave. I kept shifting position to ease the aches from the hard spots on the deck.

About a half hour later, they lowered the tarp and started to pick up the gear. Boats went up the ladder still in place offshore and went forward toward the foc's'le. As the others came up the ladder carrying the hoses, I realized that the oxyacetylene bottles and welder had been on deck between number two and number three hatches, and they had only run the hoses into the hatch.

Boats returned carrying a small and a large bucket just as they were coming up. He said something to the others and started down the ladder. When he was even with the coaming, Roy handed him the larger of the buckets, and Boats climbed down and set it on the cargo. He climbed up and repeated it with the smaller bucket, carefully holding the bucket out to the side. Walking over to the rewelded area, he started to wipe it down, and I realized he was cooling it off with water. After about fifteen minutes of that, he wiped the bulkhead with a cloth. Dipping into the smaller bucket, he started to paint the coaming.

Time to leave, the show obviously over. I had a zillion questions but no one to ask.

Backing away from the edge, I stood up and creakily stretched and then crept down the ladders to the main deck. Now I understood why no one was tending the gangway. They didn't want any witnesses, and no crew member would ever question the authority of the bosun.

I stepped out onto the gangway platform and stomped a few times as if hurrying up. I stepped on deck and went directly to my cabin, where I proceeded to worry like a dog at a bone for the next couple of hours, finally drifting off to sleep around 0100 hours.

Tony wasn't around the next morning, of course, and I'm not sure I would have confided in him anyway. I felt like I would burst if I didn't talk to someone about the events of last night.

As I walked my rounds, I took a good look at the rewelded area. While it was obvious that that particular section was freshly painted, there were a number of other areas around the coaming that had been touched up recently. I couldn't help but think that the bosun had done that ahead of time to provide cover for what would have otherwise blatantly stuck out. I also noticed a few wet stains on the crates directly under the rewelded area that must have come from the bosun soggying the coaming before he painted it.

Both elbows on the coaming, staring into space, I suddenly recalled the conversation between the captain and the mate at the beginning of the trip and how adamant the captain was that the shipyard workers be kept away from number three hatch. Whatever was going on, the captain was obviously in on it.

Knocking on the captain's door, the chief mate entered after hearing "come in," and asked the captain what he wanted to do with the twenty cases of beer they had saved. These were Sapporo, a Japanese brand. All of the others were American beers. The captain told him to give them to the purser to put in with the ship store supplies. He had already told the purser they were his personal stock and not to be sold to the crew. Knowing that the captain rarely drank beer, the mate wondered why he would bother to save twenty cases but he wasn't about to question him. He went and had the bosun deliver the beer to the purser.

We set sea watches at noon, with a planned sailing time of 1800 hours. It was closer to 1900 hours when we finally let go the last line and headed down the bay.

Chapter 10

NEWPORT NEWS

We arrived at the dock at 0630 hours, it being an eleven-hour run down the bay. There was no rush because it was Sunday, and no work was planned for that day. I thought about going ashore, but this was a navy town, so I didn't bother. Let the sailors have first dibs on the locals. Instead, I just catnapped and brooded all day about what had transpired in Baltimore.

Monday morning, 0800 hours, and we were hitting it hard with four gangs working. We were loading army six-bys. Nothing extraordinary, just a truck painted army green. They were all empty and destined for the Brazilian army as part of our AID program, or at least the part of it that applied to military equipment. The only thing to check was whether they had drained the fuel tanks down to under a quarter of a tank and to make sure they disconnected the batteries. The battery leads were taped to avoid accidental contact.

The trucks were stowed facing fore and aft to lessen the chance of break-ing loose in a heavy seaway. A ship typically rolls a lot more than it pitches, so the wheels face the direction of the least amount of movement. To start securing, the wheels were all boxed in. Typically, the wood butchers would use four-by-fours to build a box encasing the bottom of the tires. They would then place four-by-four braces between the trucks and from the trucks to the bulkheads. This made a very effective solid block of bracing that prevented the trucks from moving on the deck. They were also lashed. You can never be too secure when at sea. The mate had insisted they be lashed with wires and turnbuckles instead of the rope Spanish windlasses. The six-bys were just a little too heavy to trust to rope. Besides, the mate really didn't want to have to send someone into the hold every day while at sea to check on the Spanish windlasses, which were more susceptible to stretching and loosening than wires and turnbuckles. He said that the POVs in the upper tween deck would be okay after the first two days of stretching and tightening because they were a lot lighter and didn't "work" as much in a seaway as the trucks did.

We were also loading cigarettes into the lockers in number three upper tween deck. The mate insisted on having me or Tony at the locker door the entire time we were loading. He wasn't a trusting soul, but after working the specials, as we called them, it was clear he was right to be so careful. I made a lot of notations for the cargo report to the stevedoring company. There were over fifty cases that had been opened, with a carton or two missing from each.

It was amazing how those cartons could just open up by themselves between the time they were placed on the stevedore tray on the pier alongside and when they were stowed in the locker. The other interesting thing was that here it was, June 20 in Norfolk, and the longshoremen working in the cigarette hatch were wearing long winter overcoats. Having grown up on the waterfront in Southie, I knew that those coats all had large pockets sewn into the inside of them that were just right for holding a carton or two of cigarettes or maybe a bottle of booze. After we buttoned up the hatches, the mate told me that the count wasn't nearly as bad as he'd seen on prior trips. A matter of perspective, I guess.

We sailed at 1200 hours on Tuesday for Savannah.

Chapter 11

SAVANNAH

The most noticeable thing about our arrival in Savannah was the acrid smell from the wood pulp mills. It was in the river itself, pervasive and strong. The water was such a dingy brown you felt could shovel it instead of pour it. Drinking it was out of the question. Coming up the river, I saw a group of kids swimming in the shallows near the riverbank. Even though we were only doing ten knots, the bow wave that washed onto the riverbank was enough to provide some short-lived bodysurfing for the kids. I heard them shouting and laughing. There's no way I would have been swimming in that water. We docked at 1800 hours on Wednesday. No work was planned for that night.

Interesting history, Savannah. Being a maritime-oriented guy, I knew the first nuclear-powered commercial ship was named after the city. Beyond that, my knowledge was limited. Greg and I were talking after lunch, and he filled in some gaps in my civil rights education, as well as a good bit of the history of Savannah.

"Georgia was the last of the thirteen colonies, but Savannah, its epicenter, was designed by James Edward Oglethorpe so as to embody science, humanism, and secular government, the only colony to do so. The Oglethorpe plan envisioned social equity and social virtue using the mechanics of equitable

land allocation, stable land tenure, secular administration, yeoman gover-
nance, and prohibition of slavery. Sort of ironic since even today the South is
considered a stumbling block in the path of social justice."

Going on, he explained how the physical parameters of Savannah were
also unique for that period in time.

"The physical layout of the city, using squares as building blocks, with
each square containing residences, commercial buildings, and a central park
area, was unique then and was considered a masterpiece at the time. The basic
unit was the ward. Wards consisted of four residential blocks called tything
blocks, containing ten houses and four civic known as trust or commercial
blocks built around a central square that was a communal space."

"What made it so different from any other town?" I asked.

"A couple of things. Since the central squares were for everyone's use, the
buildings on the commercial and residential lots were designed to maximize
the size of the building and not worry about what is now called 'open space.'
The central square took care of that. Each tything, presumably ten families,
was assigned a square mile of farmland outside of town for farming, with
each family working about forty-five acres. They were also assigned a five-acre
kitchen garden closer to town. They also trained together in the local militia.
Nothing like that had ever existed before in the colonies."

"How do you know all this?" I asked.

"I got interested in civil rights, where it has been and where it is going.
You know, many of the strongest civil rights leaders came from Savannah
or nearby here. Ralph Mark Gilbert in the late forties and fifties, Mercedes
Arnold, Hosea Williams, Earl Shinhoster."

I'd never heard of any of them.

"Are you an advocate for civil rights at home?" I asked.

"I haven't been, but the more I learn, the more I'm considering it."

After thinking about it, I asked, "Why do you put up with Roy's antics
and the way he always baits you?"

Looking directly at me, he said, "Because he's a constant reminder to me
that there's a razor-thin line between joking around and true bigotry, and
it doesn't take much for anyone to cross that line. His thinly veiled bigotry

forces me to analyze how people say things and not just what they say. He forces me to keep things in the proper context. I don't always like it, but I accept it for what it is, a test of my character."

"I don't know that I could keep my cool the way you do if he said those things about me."

"You're not a black man. You couldn't possibly know how to react."

"That's true. I'm as lily white as you can get, but that doesn't mean I don't know when I'm being put down or insulted. If I was Negro, I'd be pretty pissed off."

"That's the difference between you and Roy. Roy was raised to believe that all black people were inferior to the white man. Not necessarily bad, but inferior. It's hard to know whether he's trying to overcome his built-in bigotry or just trying to show it in public in a way that won't get him in fights. In other words, he always tries to make a joke of it. I like to think he's trying to overcome his bigotry, so I give him the benefit of the doubt."

"But—" I started.

He held up his hand and stopped me.

"You, by your own admission, are simply ignorant of what a black man lives through every day. For instance, the new term for us today is 'black,' not 'Negro.' Only ignorant white people and very old black pastors call us Negro."

Seeing the red rise in my face, he threw his hands up, saying, "Ignorant means you don't know any better. I'm not insulting you—you already admitted it."

"Yeah, okay."

"You come from a ghetto. It just happened to be a white ghetto. Like anyone I've ever met who comes from that kind of background, first and foremost you don't trust strangers. It may or may not matter what color their skin is, but that's secondary to their being strangers in the neighborhood. Am I right?"

A bit taken aback at his bluntness, I hesitated a few seconds and then replied, "Yeah, you're right. Anyone coming into the neighborhood was the enemy until it was proven otherwise."

"There you go. I don't feel threatened by and I don't get mad at people like you even though their first reaction may be so standoffish. I wait until there's interaction, and then I see how they perform before I make any judgment."

Pushing the limit now, I asked, "Well, we've had interaction. Where do I stand?"

"Not too bad for white Irish trash," he said, immediately holding up his hand and laughing. "Just kidding you! Man, you should have seen the look on your face just then. What I just said, 'white Irish trash,' is something that Roy would say. You can't argue with 'white' or 'Irish,' but 'trash' set you off, didn't it? You got a low boiling point. You'd never make it as a black man. You'd either shoot someone or get shot! You're okay," he said laughingly. "You just need to fill in the gaps in your education."

"Well, I'm glad I meet your standards."

"Whoa!" he said, laughing again. "I didn't say you lived up to my standards. I just meant there's hope for you."

I sheepishly grinned and, shaking my head, slunk away, realizing just how right he was.

That night I had dinner sitting at the bar in a small restaurant. Right up until I closed the door behind me, the stench of the river was pervasive. Inside, the food aromas blotted it out. I wondered if the water they cooked with also retained that taste or smell. Striking up a conversation with a local guy sitting next to me, I asked him whether there was any relief from the odor coming from the pulp mills. With a straight face, he looked at me and said, "What odor?"

I harkened back to growing up in Southie under the airport landing approaches and the sounds of the planes and realized he was right. If it's always there, you tune it out. After dinner I went for a walk along the old town section of the waterfront. Old cotton warehouses in disrepair. It was pretty run down. In a couple of spots, it looked like they were trying to refurbish some of the places. I don't know if they were doing it to preserve it for historical purposes or trying for some commercial development. In a way, it typified what Greg was talking about earlier, an old place trying to change and adapt to new ways. Atlanta. A city not quite sure what direction it was heading. An aging actress badly in need of a facelift, maybe?

Chapter 12

───⊱✦⊰───

JACKSONVILLE

The Saint Johns River stank every bit as bad as Savannah. The first thing that hit was the pulp mill stench. There was no difference since I had spent the first week of my youngie (first year) cruise there in dry dock. That was all bad memories.

Dad died on January 2, 1964, the day of departure from Buzzards Bay on the annual training cruise. Mostly, I remember standing off in the corner at the funeral home, feeling invisible, watching all the people come and pay their respects. I did all my crying late at night, alone, eating little and sleeping less. When it was all over, I said good-bye to Ma and hopped a bus to Jacksonville, a twenty-four-hour trip. When I arrived it was around 2000 hours. Taking a cab from the bus station direct to the shipyard, I checked in with the officer of the watch and hit the sack. At 0600 the next morning, reveille sounded. Rolling out of the bunk, I stood up and passed out cold. When I came to, the pharmacist's mate, Tony, was kneeling over me, a stethoscope to my chest, telling someone to call for an ambulance. That's when I got scared. I started to ask him what was going on, but all I got from him was a sickly grin and a "Be quiet! Just relax. We'll take care of you."

Four of my classmates carried me to sick bay on a stretcher basket and left me there. Just outside the door, I heard Tony talking with someone and realized it was the captain. I couldn't believe what I was hearing!

"But, Captain, I think he's had a heart attack. When I first reached him, I couldn't detect any pulse at all. Even now, it's irregular."

"I doubt it's that serious. In any case, no one leaves this ship without being in proper uniform. Dress him!"

And so it was that I was dressed in my dress blues, lying on a litter in sick bay, and carried that way, complete with my high-pressure cap lying on my chest, to the ambulance at the foot of the gangway.

By the time the ambulance arrived at the navy hospital, I was feeling perfectly fine. After I related to the doctor the sequence of events for the prior week, he simply said I was overtired and needed exercise and two strong cups of coffee (for the caffeine) to jump-start me. His words, not mine. He then released me. Walking out through the emergency room door, I saw the medic who had brought me in the ambulance. He asked me how I was, and I explained the doctor's opinion. He chuckled. "How are you getting back to the ship?"

"I guess I'll take a cab."

"Nah, we can do better than that. Wait here."

In a minute he returned with an MP. "This is Joe Ringwald. He'll give you a ride back."

Shaking hands with Joe, I said, "I really appreciate this."

"No problem. We all know what it's like to need a friend in a strange port."

Thirty-five minutes later he dropped me off at the foot of the gangway.

We made good time going up the river. The pilot acted like he had a speedboat under him. The channel draft was thirty-four feet, and we were drawing less than twenty-eight feet, freshwater, so he wasn't worried about scraping the bottom.

This was our shortest time in port so far, memorable only in that I met up with one of my classmates, and we went to a social club and hooked up with a couple of local ladies. A lot of drinking was involved, and we decided around midnight we'd each go our separate ways with our respective girls. The one with me, Katherine—I never got her last name—was pretty drunk, so I ended up driving her car back to her apartment.

As she fumbled with the key in the lock, I leaned over and kissed her neck, resulting in a giggling fit and her dropping the key. I picked it up and unlocked the door.

"Shh! My roommate's probably asleep, and I don't want to wake her. We share a lot, but I'm not sharing you."

Grinning, she grabbed my hand and guided me into the room. Without the lights on, I could still make out the outline of a TV, a chair, and a large sofa from the light coming through the window. Leading me to the sofa, Katherine took command and pushed me down on it, sticking her tongue deep into my mouth. Disengaging, she said, "Wait a minute. I'll be right back."

I took the opportunity to adjust the sudden tightness in my shorts and kick out of my shoes.

When she returned a few minutes later, she was wearing a Mother Hubbard pullover nightgown that billowed as she moved. Standing over me, she slowly lifted the front of it up to her chin, smiled, and said, "If you're a good boy, you get this tonight. Are you a good boy?"

"No! I'm a bad boy, but I have good intentions."

"Close enough," she breathed and, still holding the nightgown in one hand, leaned over, clasped the back of my head with the other hand, and pulled my lips to her right breast, murmuring, "Start here."

More than happy to oblige, nibbling and licking her nipple, I moved on to the left breast, at the same time gently squeezing both of them.

Sighing, she pulled back a little and said, "Stand up."

Katherine then proceeded to remove my shirt and pants, running her hands over my chest and down the sides of my legs. When I reached to lower my skivvies, she caught my hands and slowly slid her fingers under the elastic and worked them down my legs, crouching down as she did. When she reached the level of my cock, she dropped the shorts, reached up and cupped my balls, then flicked her tongue over the head of my cock. I almost came right then.

She obviously knew how close I was and must have felt the same because she stopped, stood up, and whispered, "The first one is going to be fast, so let's try a little sixty-nine and save the best for later."

Without any further coaching, I lay back on the coach and let her straddle me. As she lowered her head to my cock, I pulled her hips down and plunged my tongue as far as it could go into her, then focused on her clit, causing her to shudder. Within a minute, we were both quivering like Jell-O as we had simultaneous orgasms. For a few minutes, we stayed like that, nibbling and licking. Finally, she lifted herself off and went into the bathroom. Coming back, Katherine lay down beside me, snuggled in, and promptly fell asleep. By this time, the onset of a hangover headache was appearing, and the arm that was under her was going dead, but it was a small price to pay for the pleasure I had just enjoyed.

After about an hour, Katherine woke. Nuzzling my nipple, she gently cupped my balls and rhythmically squeezed them. It was amazingly erotic and within twenty seconds, I had a raging hard-on.

"Now for the good one," she said. Hitching up her nightgown, she eased herself onto my cock ever so slowly.

"Let's make this last a really long time," she said, and then proceeded to slowly fuck my brains out.

Around 0600 hours, I awoke with a monstrous headache. Telling Katherine that I had to get back to the ship and after agreeing to meet her that night, I stumbled out of the apartment, found a cab and got back in time to go on duty at 0800 hours. The mate saw me come in for a cup of coffee and in a stage whisper said, "You look like shit, William! I hope it was worth it." I just grunted, drank the coffee down, and slithered out on deck.

We had berthed downtown at the Talleyrand municipal pier. The loading went okay, and by noon I was beginning to feel almost human again. The mate and Tony each made a few more comments at my expense at lunch as I sat there and drank water and ate some crackers. But it was deserved, so I just rolled with it. The sailing board was set for 2300 hours. I knew I wasn't going back to see Katherine and that I would most likely never see her again. I felt guilty because I had lied to her. Damn conscience.

After we had cast off and the crew finished stowing away the mooring lines, I went up to the flying bridge and watched the passing shoreline. Once away from the lights of the city, visibility reduced, but I could still hear the slap of the waves caused by the wake of the ship as they sloughed onto the riverbank. I was excited again. We were going foreign! I stayed there until we passed the sea buoy, the last marker on the river, then went to my room, cleaned up, and waited for the ordinary to call for the midwatch. Another phase of my life had begun.

Again sitting in the captain's office, the mate was fidgety as he listened.

"Well, Dennis, we never heard from Sarge's man in New York. I don't know if that means he wrote us off or he just couldn't connect, but it's up to us to decide what to do. Looks as though we're stuck unless you want to take a chance on dumping it overboard somewhere between the equator and Rio."

The mate replied, "That means we'd have to open the hatch. We can burn out the coaming without much risk of fire. We did it before but it will take at least an hour to open the hatch and burn the hole. Then at least another half hour to get the stuff out and dump it. We'd have to do it between four thirty and six thirty a.m. to keep either of the thirds from seeing what's going on. Even then, one of them might be awake and see something."

"That would still be the most prudent thing to do."

"Gawd damn, Captain, I hate to just toss it all over the side. We went to a lot of trouble getting all this arranged. Why don't we just let it sweat and see where they'll send us after this trip?"

"Okay, Dennis, let's just think about it for now."

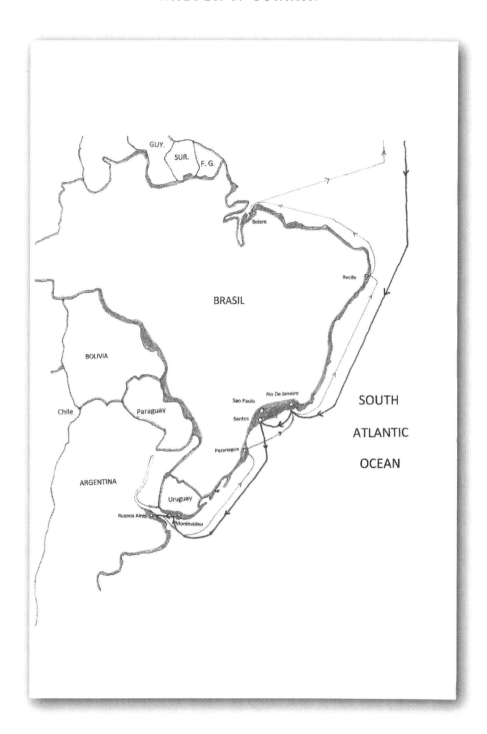

Chapter 13

SEA PASSAGE

All the way through the Caribbean and down into the South Atlantic, the weather was near perfect. Except for an occasional afternoon squall, it was classic postcard weather.

I had been in the Caribbean on all of my training cruises, so there was nothing new. But the same feeling of belonging came over me when I was alone on watch. The brightness of the azure sky backlit the intermittent fair-weather cumulus clouds as they skittered along. A heavy salt aroma and constant blanket of humidity kept wrapping me in its embrace.

During the day, enhanced by the clarity of the water, the dolphins blazed the trail for our bow. Their acrobatics and flying fish skittering away from our perceived pursuit supplied the entertainment during an otherwise boring watch.

At night, the phosphorescence on the bow waves caused by the ship cutting through the water created a show worthy of Disneyland. It was a wet aurora borealis, and it never failed to mesmerize me.

Often, I would find myself startled as if I had drifted off to sleep. But it wasn't sleep, it was reverie, my mind wafting away to parts unknown, only to be shaken and roused by a gust of wind or slap of a wave against the hull. It was, in a word, serene.

The few afternoons that we got a local squall, the sequence was always similar. The cloud buildup would start around 1400 hours. By 1700 hours, somewhere on our perimeter there would be a headwall of cumulonimbus clouds blotting out the sun. Soon thereafter, the wind would start to gust, followed by a solid sheet of water slamming into the ship. At other times, we could follow the progress of the squall, but it was on the horizon, and the squall never reached us. One time we were in a triangle of squalls. One was on our port quarter, another on our starboard quarter, and a third was straight ahead of us, each streaking lightning and spewing thunder. Those were three angry storms! The smell of ozone was immensely strong, but not one drop of rain struck us that day. It was bizarre.

While we had a mostly calm passage, the captain reminded me one day that the Caribbean was the maritime equivalent of Tornado Alley in the great plains of the mainland. Recounting one of his experiences, he told me about a hurricane he had sailed into.

"Late September, it was. Typically, this storm started in mid-Atlantic as a tropical depression. The weather data we were getting indicated it was slow moving, and we should have been able to sail out of its path. Instead, the storm sped up and intensified into a category two hurricane. By the time we got the radio data and made our weather chart, we were committed. It was safer to proceed than go back. The ship would be on the southern side of the storm—the southwest quadrant, which is less of a danger. The worst part is the northeast quadrant."

I knew because of my studies in meteorology that cyclones spin counterclockwise in the Northern Hemisphere and clockwise in the Southern Hemisphere due to the Coriolos effect. If you want to know where the eye of the cyclone is, face the wind, extend your right arm at a right angle to your body, and you are pointing at the eye.

Interrupting his story, the captain asked the helmsman, the ship being on autopilot, to go get him a cup of coffee.

"As the storm approached, the wind and seas rose, coming from the port beam, working around to the port quarter. When the waves got to twenty feet, I had to make a decision. We were corkscrewing badly, so I decided to head into the wind rather than run with it dead on our stern. There was too much chance of our getting 'pooped' by a big sea if I ran away from it. Turning the ship was dicey. The timing had to be good to minimize the roll when we were momentarily broadside to the waves, but we made it okay.

"Once the wave height reached thirty feet, I slowed down enough to just maintain headway. I didn't want to be slamming into the seas but had to maintain steerage. We rode it out for about fifteen hours. By then the seas were dropping but still had an occasional thirty footer. It was then I decided that we could resume our course and get back on schedule."

Pointing to the inclinometer on the forward bulkhead, the captain asked, "What's the maximum list on that?"

The inclinometer is simply a plumb bob with an upside-down clock face. It shows how many degrees the ship is listing or rolling at any given time. Zero degrees is at the bottom, and it goes up to fifty-two degrees on both the left and right. At fifty-two degrees there is a little peg that doesn't allow the needle to go any farther. The reason is that no one expects to recover from a fifty-two-degree roll.

"Fifty-two degrees, Captain," I responded.

"We were about a quarter of the way into our turn when the helmsman said, 'Holy shit!' Looking up, I saw there was a rogue wave coming at us that had to be at least sixty feet high. There was no turning back. I told the helmsman, 'Keep it hard over,' then grabbed onto the ball at the binnacle and held tight. I stared at the inclinometer and saw it peg at fifty-two degrees."

"What did you do?" I asked.

"Nothing. I thought we were goners for sure, but the old girl just sort of shuddered and rolled back up. Once we completed the turn, we were fine."

"Was the ship damaged?"

"Other than a mess down in the galley, she held up fine."

The helmsman returned then and handed the captain his coffee.

"Fair weather is a seaman's best friend, sonny." And with that, he walked off the bridge.

Crossing the equator was almost a nonevent. Tony and I were the only ones on board that hadn't crossed the line, so we were expecting to get a raft of shit from the old timers. But unlike the navy and training ship, with their tradition of kissing Neptune's belly and other less savory tactics, this was the real world. All we got was some kidding from the mate and chief about being pollywogs. We were almost disappointed.

Chapter 14

RIO

We were heading almost due north, passing Cabo de São Tomé and heading for Cabo Frio, where we would make the turn in toward Rio. Smell of land had been in the air for two days, an exotic scent that seemed to be a mixture of coffee, cocoa, jungle rot, and other indefinable odors. Around 1300 hours, Cabo Frio was abeam off to starboard, and we changed course to 270 degrees. When Ponta Negra was abeam to starboard, I had the ordinary seaman call the captain as per his orders. The captain came up to the bridge and asked him our position. I told him we were about twenty miles east of the pilot station and that we had radar and visual plots. There were three other ships, two ahead and one slightly abaft of the port beam, all heading into the pilot station.

Calling down to the engine room, the captain ordered them to drop to maneuvering speed, which for us was about eighteen knots. The engineers could add a couple of nozzles and take it as high as twenty-one and a half knots when pressed.

Walking out to the starboard wing, the captain turned and spoke toward me rather than to me, as he so often did, and said, "It's the smell you remember. No matter how long you've been away, when normal recollection fails, that smell will hit you, and it will come back as if it were just yesterday."

Turning away, he stared off at the land, somewhat blurred and indistinct to the eye, but perfectly tuned in to the nose. Two hours later, having slowed to five knots, we made an easy turn to 310 degrees and headed toward the pilot boat.

When the second relieved me at 1600 hours, the captain was still on the starboard wing. As a courtesy, I went out and informed him that I was relieved and, in a sycophantic mood, asked him if he would like a cup of coffee or anything before I went below.

"No, thanks, sonny," he responded.

Going below to my cabin, I was unable to sit still. So I went up on deck to a gentle onshore breeze and stared westward at a coastline silhouetted by the setting sun. Off the starboard bow was the pilot boat just approaching the ship. To the right of that was the entrance to Rio's harbor. To the left was the celestial image of Cristo Redentor—Christ the Redeemer—perched on Corcovado overlooking Guanabara Bay and overshadowing Sugarloaf Mountain at its right. Scattered below was the city.

An awe-inspiring and peaceful setting at that time of day, the only incongruous site was half a dozen forty-foot cargo containers dotting the hillside like bungalows. At first, I thought it was advertising because all the containers had a steamship line name on them. But when I got the binoculars on them, I realized they were being used as housing. Welcome to Rio!

By 1700 hours, we had taken the pilot on board. At 1800 hours, the captain called us out to mooring stations. The tugs were the largest I had ever seen, half again the size of the tugs I had seen in the States. I had no idea whether they had more horsepower, but they were certainly built on a massive scale. Their towing platforms were big enough to run sprints on. Except for the tugs, it was no different from docking in any other port.

The stevedores worked Saturday, but the mate said they wouldn't work on Sunday. He gave me and Tony the day off, saying he'd watch the store if we wanted to go ashore.

I told Tony I was going to head over to Ipanema and check out the girls. He wanted to go sightseeing, so we ended up going our separate ways. I checked with Greg, but he passed on it too. Laughing, he warned me, "These folks are a little darker than you're used to, white boy. Better be careful!"

By this time I was used to his banter and was getting to like him more and more each day. I said, "I'll try not to disgrace my race," and left the ship.

Ipanema…a dream fantasy come to life.

Not sure if I'd be able to find a place to change, I decided to just wear my bathing suit under my pants and stuffed a set of skivvies and a towel into my small duffel bag. Grabbing an extra pack of Marlboros, I headed out for Ipanema.

In the song, Frank Sinatra had made the place a legend and every man's dream of where to find the perfect woman. I was determined to find that perfect woman. After all, I was twenty-one, not bad looking (in my opinion), and ready to bestow my favors upon the world. The least the world could do was grant my wish.

I caught a cab at the terminal gate, and it took about twenty-five minutes and three thousand cruzeiros to reach the beach. That sounds like an expensive taxi ride, but the exchange rate was about two thousand cruzeiros to the dollar. There was a guy selling Coca-Cola out of a kiosk on wheels, and I bought one; it came in a smaller bottle than what they use in the States. Kicking off my shoes, I walked barefoot down the beach.

It was pretty crowded, even for a Sunday, mostly with young mothers and not-so-young grandmothers and grandfathers watching over hundreds of three- to four-year-old human sand fleas. Disappointment was rapidly setting in since the only nubile bodies evident had kids attached to them. Deciding that the day wouldn't go to waste, I stripped down to my bathing suit, jammed my clothes into the duffel, and carried it down close to the waterline so I could watch it. Getting a running start, I porpoised over one wave and ran smack into the following one. It felt great! I started to swim out and then thought better of it, afraid to lose sight of my clothes. So I splashed around in water up to my chest for about fifteen minutes. Wading ashore, I spread the towel out and lay down to catch some rays. Nothing beats the feel of hot sun baking your back while you belly hump and punch the sand to get a comfortable position. At heart, I am a true beach bum.

Just as I was coughing up some saltwater dregs, I sensed and then saw these two pillars of flesh appear before me. Looking up, I realized they were attached to a very fat woman. She wore a one-piece bathing suit that was stretched beyond all normal limits of endurance; it was so tight that the fabric itself looked almost translucent in some places. She was smiling at me and saying hello in surprisingly good English. In the time it took to take a deep breath, my reactions ran from shock to disappointment to fear that someone would see me with her and then to anger at what shitty luck I had. In other words, I behaved like a stupid teenager.

"*Bom dia*," I muttered, using up half my Portuguese vocabulary in the process.

"You are American?" she asked, stepping a little closer and causing a personal eclipse of the sun.

"Yes...*Si*...I'm American."

"My name is Claudia," she said, pronouncing it *Clowdia*. She then asked, "Are you here on holiday?" which is the way they refer to vacation.

"No. I'm working, but I have the day off."

She settled into the sand, sitting Indian fashion and proving to be amazingly agile for someone so big.

"What is your name?" she asked.

I was having a hard time concentrating on her words, though, because in settling into the sand, she had positioned herself so that her crotch, or at least what could be seen of it behind the thickness of her thighs, was staring me directly in the face at a distance of less than two feet. It was not the least bit enticing. Instead, it was disconcerting.

Rolling over and sitting up, I finally stammered, "*Me llamo William*," forgetting entirely that she was speaking English and that the native language was Portuguese, not Spanish. Being somewhat less than a linguist, my first impression of Portuguese was that it was Spanish spoken with a German accent.

"William, William," she said, repeating it to herself. "That is not American name, no?"

"Yes, it is."

"Huh," she grunted, neither agreeing nor disagreeing. "Claudia is Italiano name. You know Italiano?"

"You mean Italian?" I asked, immediately displaying my ignorance by correcting the language of a girl who apparently could speak at least two more languages than I could.

"Yes." She smiled. "Italian."

Just then, two little boys about three years old came running over yelling, "Clowdy," at the top of their voices. Gently shushing them, she said something to cause them to look at me, then shrink away and hide behind her, an easy thing, given their relative size.

"They seem to be afraid of me."

"They not afraid. They"—she groped for the word in English—"shy. Yes, shy! Indicating first the one on her left and then nodding to the other, she said, "This is Paulo, and this is Alejandro." They just continued to peek out at me.

"Are they your kids…you know, children?"

Laughing, she shook her head no. "I am a pear." She paused and said, "Babysitting? No?"

Well, I knew what a babysitter was but didn't have the foggiest notion why she called herself a pear. I didn't think she was referring to her overall shape, though the description was pretty accurate.

While I was pondering her choice of words, she leaned forward and began to rise, and I was treated to the Grand Canyon of cleavage. She caught me staring, gave me a little smile, and said, "I must go."

Taking the kids by the hand, she sashayed down the beach, twitching that mighty rump so it appeared to be two bulldogs battling in a burlap sack. Despite her size, she exuded sex appeal. I felt more than a little horny but thought better about chasing after her to see where it could lead. Instead, I just ran into the water again, a lukewarm equivalent of a cold shower.

I was starting to feel the sun and walked up to the street to a small *farmacia*. They had all the usual things with a lot of strange names. An old standby caught my eye: Coppertone. That baby's lily-white ass was popular even down here, so I bought a small bottle.

Back on the beach side of the boulevard, I greased up, wiped my hands in the sand, and bought a soda from a street vendor. Meandering over to sit under a palm tree, I nursed the soda while trying not to be too obviously a *tourista*.

As the afternoon wore on, the parade of people along the boulevard increased, with the preponderance being teenagers. The boys were, for the most part, average looking, in good shape, and dark-skinned. The girls were all strikingly beautiful, and I was surprised to see a number of blondes and redheads with fair skin. They all caught my eye, and it was clear that bikinis were the in thing, because most of the delectable young things were wearing them. Notwithstanding their obvious physical attributes, what I found most striking was that they had such an air of confidence. Not the guys. They behaved like typical teenage boys: a little too pushy and a little too noisy. Unlike the shrieky, gawky teenage girls at home, these girls seemed, at least to this unpolished guy, sophisticated.

Even as I was thinking this, I questioned myself.

"How can you say they're sophisticated? You haven't said a word to any of them, and you can't understand what they're saying to one another."

Nevertheless, that was the impression I came away with: sophisticated. Needless to say, when I was right there in a world of pretty girls and all I could do was have an argument with myself and lose, I was pretty hard up.

Deciding to check out what appeared to be a small piazza a half mile away, I brushed away as much sand as I could, wiped the salt off my back with my towel, and strolled down the beach. Crossing the boulevard, I was pulling my shirt on as I passed the entryway to a large apartment building. Just then, I heard, "*Hola*, William!"

It was her, big girl, Claudia.

"Hi." I smiled, utterly at a loss for words. "Where are the kids, the children?"

"They are with Mama. I am, how you say, not on duty."

"Off duty?"

"*Si! Si!* Off duty," she said laughingly.

It was a nice laugh and an impish smile. She was wearing what appeared to me to be a large purple towel that was wrapped around her a few times. Although it couldn't hide her size, it did seem to smooth out the lines of her shape to the point where they transitioned from fat to overly voluptuous.

"What do you do?" she asked.

I was puzzled for a second. Then I realized she was asking me what I was doing.

"Just looking around. Maybe get something to eat. It's almost suppertime."

"What is suppertime?" she asked.

"Dinner. *La comida?*"

"Ah! *Jantar!* Too soon for *jantar*, dinner. We eat dinner at nine or ten o'clock."

"I'll never make it. I haven't had any lunch, and I'm getting hungry."

Grabbing my hand, she started to move off, saying, "I show you *botequim* with small foods."

I took this to mean snacks like peanuts or potato chips and just let her lead me along.

One block down and two blocks back from the beach, we came to a small restaurant/bar called Bombeiros, which is "firefighter" in Portuguese. It had a twenty-foot-long bar, maybe six small tables, and was completely empty. Walking in, she called out something. After a minute, a little guy who could have passed for the twin of Charlie Chaplin came out of the back room. Seeing her, his face lit up.

"Claudia!" he shouted and gave her a hug and kissed her on both cheeks. It was pretty clear that she was either a relative or a regular at the bar. Turning to me, she introduced us.

"William, this is my very good friend Raoul. Raoul, this is my new friend, William. He is an Americano."

"Hello, Senor William," he said, followed by a couple of short sentences in Portuguese, none of which I caught.

"Nice to meet you," I replied.

"It's okay," Claudia said. "You don't need talk to Raoul. I talk for two of us." Then she let fly that infectious laugh again.

Commandeering the corner table, sort of a half-booth arrangement, she pushed me in first and then slid in beside me, all the time telling me that she would order some small foods. I ordered a Cuba libre, and she ordered something I had never heard of. When the drinks arrived, I asked her what she was drinking.

Handing me the glass, she said, "Drink it."

Taking a small sip, I decided that it was akin to a rusty nail. That's a combination of booze I avoided, so I smiled politely and just handed it back to her.

Feeling a little uncomfortable, I raised my glass and said, "To you, Claudia, my new friend."

You'd think I had just proclaimed her queen of England.

Gasping, she clutched my free hand and said, "You are very nice!"

Downing her drink in one swallow, she smiled brightly and called for another. I began to get that hair-rising-at-the-nape-of-the-neck feeling. I ignored it and continued to socialize.

Claudia was an extremely animated talker, with not only her hands moving in sync with her lips, but her whole body seeming to shimmy and shake in vibrato with her voice.

The small foods arrived, and it turned out to be chorizo, a sort of blood sausage; *batata frita*, Brazil's version of french fries; and some sort of fried plantain or squash. I played with the squash, but the chorizo and *batata frita* were good.

By the time the food was gone and we had finished our third drinks, the place was starting to fill up. Patting me on the knee, Claudia said, "Wait, I go talk to Raoul."

Then she disappeared into the back room. A minute later, she came out with him. He went behind the bar, bent over, and began to fiddle with something under the bar. When the music started, I realized it was a stereo of some sort.

Striking a pose in front of the table, Claudia held out her hand and commanded, "Dance!"

It must have been the three drinks, because I didn't even do my usual "I can't dance" routine. I just got up, took her hand, and said, "Show me how."

And she did! I'm a terrible dancer, mostly because I try to concentrate too much on the actual mechanics. Claudia didn't allow that to happen. She was truly graceful. Because she was so big, the pressure and presence of her body forced me to just follow her lead. What with the food, liquid, and exercise, I had to call a time-out for a trip to the head. Claudia followed me over to the bathroom and would probably have followed me in if I hadn't closed the door on her.

After wringing the last drop from Little William, I washed my hands and face. Staring in the mirror, I wondered where this night was going and if I really wanted to go there.

Claudia was waiting for me when I emerged, and she led me back to the table. This time, when she squeezed in, she *really* squeezed in, making full contact from shoulder to ankle and casually placing her hand halfway up my thigh.

Being the sophisticated man of the world that I was, I of course immediately started to get a hard-on. Embarrassed at my lack of control, I attempted conversation.

"Why do they call this place Bombeiros? Did they name it after the local firemen?"

The reason I knew the word "firemen" is because the mate had told me at the onset of the trip to learn some basic words in Portuguese such as the words for "port," "starboard," "open the hatch," "close the hatch," etc., and the biggest emergency on a ship is fire.

"Yes! Many years ago, it was different name. But many firemen come here. The girlfriend of one fireman came here and catch her boyfriend with another woman. There was much *disparando* between the women, and the first girlfriend told the other woman, 'Keep him! With these firemen, I get a bigger hose!'" She did that half-laugh, half-giggle thing, adding, "It has been Bombeiros since then after."

She punctuated her words by running her hand all the way up my crotch and giving Little William a friendly squeeze.

It had the opposite effect of what I expected. What had a moment ago been so hard that a cat couldn't scratch it immediately faded away into mush. Just like that, the moment was over.

I told Claudia I had to return to the ship to go on duty. While clearly disappointed, she didn't go into a huff. The total tab turned out to be thirty-two thousand cruzeiros, about seventeen dollars. Incredible!

Thanking Claudia for the good time, I offered to escort her home—with the best intentions since I had walked there with her—but she declined.

"If you escort me to my bedroom, *si!*" she said with that flashing grin. "No, I walk home with girlfriends."

I was truly contrite when I told her I couldn't, but as I said, the moment had passed.

"*Tchau!*" she said and turned away.

Calling good-bye to Raoul, I went out, turned left, walked to the boulevard, and caught a cab back to the ship.

Talking with Greg over coffee, I related my adventure with Claudia, Miss Pear, in Ipanema. He suddenly burst out laughing and shouted, "Au pair! Au pair, you dope! That's French for a babysitter or nanny!" I was too embarrassed to even get mad at him for calling me a dope.

Chapter 15

SANTOS

We rounded Pta. Do Boi on Ilha de Sao Sebastiao and settled on course 270 degrees to keep clear of the Ilha de Alcatrazes and its shoals, following this all the way into the outer anchorage. After picking up the pilot, we turned to twenty-two degrees for the approach to the channel, and then the pilot took over.

The smell again! Different, yet eerily the same. The big difference between here and Rio was the color of the water. The silty outflow from the river made the blue-green ocean turn brown for a distance of about five miles, with each mile out being a different shade of brown. It ranged from baby-shit brown right at the mouth to dirty brown to sandy and then ecru before melding back into teal green. At the mouth of the river, we went past a line of oceanfront apartments. When I commented to the pilot that it reminded me of Miami Beach, he said that the area was called Guaruja and that a lot of rich people owned property there. That was soon left behind and the quasi-squalor of a river port became the norm, with its attendant transit sheds, cranes, warehouses, and dirt.

Santos is a major port in the North–South America trade. Coffee is big, but it exports other cargo: auto wheels, synthetic resins, forgings, rubber, gelatin made from beef skin. Many imports also move through here, depending on the local economy and world market conditions.

The main event on this trip was the army six-bys. Loaded in Norfolk as part of the military portion of our lend-lease program with Brazil, they required a military representative at time of discharge. An army top sergeant with the unlikely name of Huey Long—also born and raised in Louisiana—came down towing an alcoholic major behind him to sign for them. As the longshoremen unloaded them, an army private would give them a quick once-over, connect the battery, and drive the truck to the end of the pier, where they were lined up. After the trucks were all discharged, the sergeant had the major sign the receipt, and the major left. The mate invited the sergeant up for a beer, which he readily accepted.

A little later, I was going ashore with Greg to go sightseeing. The sergeant was just leaving and offered us a ride to the gate. As we passed the end of the pier where the army six-bys were, I noticed about ten men painting the trucks a bright blue. I asked the sergeant if that was the color of the Brazilian army, and he laughed.

"What's so funny?"

"Y'all must be on your first trip down here. Those trucks that the US of A so generously gave them for nothin' were just sold by the garrison commandant to a local truckin' company."

"But that's illegal!"

"All I know is, once they sign for them, my hands are clean. After that, it's none of my business."

Boy, was I was pissed off! My patriotic side was offended because, in principle, I didn't believe in government giveaway programs, but also because I now knew it was a fraud. I had been naïve enough to think things were legitimate.

The sergeant took us to the main drag and warned us that all the bars had working B-girls. If we planned on getting drunk, the only place that was relatively safe was the Blue Star Café.

"What makes it safer than any other joint?"

"The fact that it's owned by a couple of expats. One's German, and the other's American, and they tend to watch over the hometown boys. They'll still take your money, but they won't let anyone else take it while you're in their place."

Getting out, I thanked him and told him that maybe I'd see him next trip.

"Not likely. I'm getting rotated out soon and heading for Thailand. Some asshole port called Sattahip with nothing but snakes and sailors."

With that, he saluted and drove off.

Looking around, we saw a few junk shops with local curios and a bunch of bars. On the street were a half dozen or so peddlers selling what looked to be chunks of barbecued beef they were cooking on charcoal braziers. Later I found out they were referred to as puppy-dog noses. I never ate one while I was sober but sampled them once when I was a little less than sober, and they weren't bad. It's all in your attitude!

"Which way?" I asked Greg.

He just shrugged, so I pointed toward what I thought was uptown, and we ambled in that direction, walking about a block to a place called Maison Verde. Considering the national language was Portuguese, I figured a French place might have a little class. Wrong! What a shithole! Less than four steps inside the door, we were driven back out by the smell. The whole area smelled like an outhouse in summer because of the open sewer drains alongside the road, but this place had a contest going between the smell of puke and shit, and it was a dead heat.

A half block farther along, there was another place with no name at all. Because it reminded me of the No Name restaurant at the fish pier in Boston, I decided to try it. It too smelled bad but no worse than the general area. There were about a dozen patrons, half of whom looked to be foreign seamen. We decided to keep looking and went out, turning up the street.

At the next corner, we saw a sign with a picture of a big blue star and followed our instinct. It was the Blue Star Café the sergeant had told us about. I ordered a Cuba libre, and Greg ordered a beer. Looking around, I saw there was a tiny stage back in the corner with the most beat-up spinet I had ever seen and a barstool instead of a piano bench. The stool was about a foot too high for a normal person to sit on while playing. There was a huge old RCA radio behind the bar playing some kind of samba music. The bartender, a wizened old man, completely bald, was mentally dancing to the music, judging by the subtle movements of his body, but not his feet.

Turning to Greg, I said, "I just want to drink tonight, so if I start to look at any girls, haul my ass back to the ship. Okay?"

"Sure," he said laughingly. "I'll keep you pure and chaste tonight."

At the end of the bar, Greg had struck up a conversation with an engineer from a Norwegian ship. After a half hour, I was getting bored and restless and had just signaled for the bartender to pay for the drink when I was tapped on the shoulder. Turning, I saw Lucy. I didn't know her name was Lucy. Not then. That came much later, after many drinks and a lot of dancing, followed by fumbling, feeling up, and groping. No, just then it was, "Buy me drink?"

Lucy, you see, was a B-girl. B-girls worked as shills trying to get you to buy them "champagne," some god-awful liquid they poured out of a champagne bottle right after they filled it with that same god-awful liquid. Of course, they charged you extra for the so-called champagne.

The girls worked on commission. As a side benefit, for every drink you bought, you could cop a feel of either or both boobs. Think of it as a luxury tax. After the third drink, when it seemed you might be slowing down and somewhat reluctant to buy her yet another champagne, she'd accidentally grab your cock while pretending to brush something off your lap. This, along with the salubrious effects of the drinks that you were also tossing down, had the immediate desired effect of you wanting to buy her another drink just to see how far you were going to get. Ironically, other than the feeling and groping, you weren't about to get anything. Body rental was the private preserve of the A-girls, the real hookers, and they didn't want the B-girls horning in on their territory. Capitalism at its finest!

Anyway, after I bought Lucy a drink, Greg came back and whispered in my ear, "Remember, you didn't want any girls. We can go back to the ship now if you want."

"I'm all right, Greg, just going to finish my drink."

So he walked away and went back to the Norwegian.

About a half hour and another two drinks later, Greg came back and reminded me again. But by that time, I was in love and slightly belligerent and told him, "Fuck off! I don't need a babysitter!"

Being a better friend than I was, he tried one more time to get me to leave. But when I threatened to beat the shit out of him, something I undoubtedly would have failed at, given the condition I was in, he gave up and left me there.

In the end, alcohol prevailed. I passed out at the table, and, unbeknownst to me at the time, the American owner of the bar poured me into a cab and told the driver to take me back to my ship. The owner must have had a lot of clout with that cabbie. When I woke up the next morning, I was in my room on the ship. I had all of my belongings, including my money, except for about ten bucks, probably what the cabbie took as fare. I was astounded at my good fortune and then started to remember the way I had treated Greg. I went looking for him to apologize, but he just laughed and told me I wasn't the first shipmate that spurned his company for that of a hooker and that I should count my blessings that I got back at all.

Tony and I had agreed to take a whole day of watch apiece so that we could both get ashore for an entire day. I won the coin flip and opted to take Friday off, so I stood watch from 0600 hours on Thursday until 0800 hours Friday morning. It wasn't bad because the longshoremen knocked off at 2300 hours, and at midnight I just went to sleep in my cabin.

Friday morning, the daytime commotion eventually woke me, and I blearily discovered it was 0930 hours. After getting a cup of coffee and kick-starting my lungs with a cigarette, I showered, shaved, and put my bathing suit on under my dungarees. I packed a towel, suntan lotion, and a pair of skivvies to change into later into my rucksack—I hated walking around with a wet crotch—and headed for Guaruja.

It was a beautiful beach, and it was pretty crowded for a weekday. I stripped down to my bathing suit and ran into the water, careful to keep an eye on my rucksack, which I had put near the waterline. Walking back toward the strip between the beach and the high-rise buildings, I saw a bunch of kids about ten or eleven years old standing in a circle with a guy in the middle juggling a soccer ball. The guy was talking to them in Portuguese, so I didn't know what he was saying.

He seemed to be instructing them, all the while juggling the ball from his right foot to his knee, his shoulder, his head, and then the other shoulder, knee, and foot. Then he reversed the cycle, not once missing a beat. At the same time, he was slowly turning in a circle so that he faced all the kids. I played soccer in school, and although I possessed very little actual soccer skill, I could really appreciate how good he was. Approaching them, I stared at the guy. Suddenly, it dawned on me that I had seen him before. It was Pelé, the world's greatest soccer player!

I stood there with the kids for a while, and they were peppering him with questions. After a few minutes, he was facing me, and he said something to me.

"I don't speak Portuguese," I managed to stammer.

He replied in English with a heavy accent, "You play *futbol*?"

"Not good, but I love the game."

"Ha, ha! Good! Good!" he said, turning away and continuing his dialogue with the kids.

After another five minutes, he yelled something to the kids, and they all started to run down the beach. As they were running, he kicked the soccer ball toward the water, and they scrambled after it. Turning, he nodded in my direction and then trotted across the strip and went into one of the high rises.

When I related my story of meeting Pelé to the local steamship agent, he told me that Pelé owned that building and a few others.

We sailed from Santos on Saturday at 0600 hours. After dropping the pilot, we continued on course 202 degrees until we had Ilha Queimada Grande to our right on the starboard quarter bearing 336 degrees. Turning to 230 degrees, we continued until clearing Ilha do Bom Abrigo and then turned due south, generally keeping outside the fifty-fathom line.

Chapter 16

NIGHT WATCH

Night watches were different—sometimes hectic, sometimes sublime, an opportunity to marvel at the intensity of the cosmos and the sea's miraculous luminescence. Rarely is there any excitement. Lonely, yet savoring the quiet; semi-impatiently biding one's time until relief, but strangely content, the bubbling, iridescent ship's wake a nerve balm.

Preheated coffee cup a staple, habit learned from frigid nights on watch on the quarterdeck of the training ship. Seventy degrees warmer here, but no matter—real or psychological, habit is habit.

The helmsman, a shadow crossing the binnacle's glow, was intermittently enhanced by the glare of a drag on a cigarette.

Perpetual squint when peering at distant horizon, on occasion interrupted by flickering of stars or ship's lights. Initial curiosity drifting to cautious concern, I run a plot, light a cigarette, and meander back to complacency.

Deep night brings deep thoughts and deep discussions in this strangely normal world. Ordinary seamen become extraordinary philosophers. Able-bodied seamen have so many infirmities. Contradicting realities, laughable terms.

The watch usually begins and ends mundanely. The distant echo of the ordinary seaman knocking on doors is the start. Next the subtle rattle of cutlery and dishes and slurred voices as the relieving watch grazes through the midnight meal prepared earlier for them. The helmsman and I glance more frequently toward the door leading to the companionway in anticipation of relief. Finally footsteps—slow, clambering ones from the massive second mate and quick stutter steps from the young AB relieving the helmsman.

Helmsman relates course to new helmsman, informs the mate that he is relieved, nods at the incoming mate, and disappears into the red-lit glow of the companionway.

I tell the second mate the course and speed, update him on any vessel traffic, and relay any standing or special orders from the captain. Once he acknowledges the information, he tells me I'm relieved. "Good night" and I am off to the rack. In seven hours I'll repeat it all, this time with the sun.

Chapter 17

SPARKY

We were two hours away from turning the corner into the river Plate on our way to Montevideo, Monte to the old timers, when I heard strange noises coming from the back of the bridge. Telling Sturm to keep an eye out ahead, I walked back into the passageway and stood there for about ten seconds, not hearing anything. Turning back, I heard a muffled thud coming from the radio room. I walked over and knocked on the door. Not getting a response, I tried the knob. It opened, and there, hanging upside down suspended by his ankles with hands tied behind him, was Sparky.

Sparky really was an asshole, just as Roy had initially described him. The officers had taken a vote on it one night, and it was a unanimous decision.

Sparky was always losing personal messages or forgetting to send personal messages, things that were incredibly important to someone out of touch with family for three months. He was nosy as hell, and it had become pretty clear that he did it deliberately to get even with the raunchy way everyone treated him. Sparky was also continually running to the captain to complain about how he was persecuted by the rest of the officers. It was a real chicken-or-egg situation and had been going on forever. No one knew which came first, whether they started to hate Sparky because he forgot messages, or he forgot messages because they hated him. Whichever came first, it was firmly ingrained by the time I came aboard the ship.

To be fair, when Roy, the second engineer, first started to rant about Sparky, I made an attempt to see if I could get on Sparky's good side and deliberately tried to befriend him. All overtures were greeted with a shrill, "You're like the rest of them! Don't pretend you're my friend. No one's my friend!"

While saying this, he was twirling a four-inch switchblade in his hand, that he used as a letter opener, something that I later found out was a constant habit with him. The captain had forbidden him to carry it in the officers' salon, but he carried it everywhere else. Sparky's tirade was at once followed by the door slamming in my face.

So there I was, staring at him strung up from the ceiling frame he used as his back stretcher. Apparently, he had lower-back problems from sitting hunched over at the radio console all day, so he had rigged up a block-and-tackle arrangement whereby it was possible to hang himself upside down to ease the stress on his back. There was a bag over his head, and he was making noises. Pulling the bag off his head, I saw there was a gag in his mouth.

Well, I was perplexed, to say the least. Obviously he hadn't done this to himself. My first thought was, "If I release him, someone is going to be pissed off at me." After pondering the situation for about another thirty seconds, watching him stare at me with eyes agog as he strained to utter words through the gag, I walked out and closed the door behind me. I wasn't sure if the noise he made sounded more like crying or if it was just my pettiness hoping so, but I was satisfied either way.

At the same time, I had a flashback to my second-class year at MMA, when a few of us had strung up one of our classmates nicknamed Ming Toy in a similar manner because he had ratted out one of us to an upperclassman. Granted, he said he didn't mean to rat him out, but we figured that even if he didn't do it deliberately, he was too stupid to be forgiven. So we strung him up for a half hour.

Returning to the bridge, I answered Sturm's questioning look, saying, "Must have been my imagination."

Then I walked out to the wing for a smoke.

About an hour later, I called the captain as per his night orders and related our position to him. Ten minutes later, he walked onto the bridge, motioned me out to the wing with him, and said in his best stage voice, "Do I dare presume that you know nothing about Sparky hanging like a plucked chicken in his cabin?"

"What do you mean, Captain?"

"Just what I said!" he said, stressing every syllable. "Did you see or hear anything unusual during your watch?"

"No, sir, nothing at all unusual. Oh wait, about an hour ago, I thought I heard a clunking noise behind the bridge. But when I walked back, there wasn't anything there, so I chalked it up to wind noise."

The captain stared at me for about ten seconds, and I was really beginning to sweat. Finally he cleared his throat and said, "I will relieve you here on the bridge. Go to the radio room and untether Sparky."

As I turned to go, he added, "And, Mr. Connolly, when you lower him down, don't have any accidents."

"Yes, sir." I smirked and left.

Reentering Sparky's room, I saw that he wasn't moving. My first thought was, "Shit! He's had a brain hemorrhage or something hanging upside down all this time."

When I touched him, he started to jerk around, and I yelled, "Calm down! I'm letting you down!"

It was a bitch to untie the knot at the top of the block because his twitching had jammed it so tight. I was forced to cut it with my knife. The line running through the sheaves slowed his drop somewhat, but even with my holding onto him, his head hit pretty hard on the deck. I then cut the rope on his hands and stepped back. I didn't know whether he was going to attack me or what, but he just took the gag out of his mouth, rubbed his hands, and started to cry. That took me by surprise. I started to feel bad, but I just left and went back to the bridge.

"Is he all right?" the captain asked.

"I think so, sir. When I left, he was sitting on the deck crying."

"Damned overgrown kids!" he muttered. "Wake up the steward, and have him go see if Sparky needs any medical attention."

"Aye, aye, Captain." And off I went.

Chapter 18

MONTEVIDEO

Dropping off sea speed, we were about ten miles south-southeast of Isla de Lobos. When the light bore 342 degrees, we changed to 279 degrees and headed for the outer approaches to Montevideo. The channel to Monty is about twenty-three miles long and fairly narrow—approximately 2,500 feet wide—but it was well marked with lighted buoys. At the end of the approach channel, we turned due north all the way through the breakwaters and maneuvered into the berthing areas shown as Darsena I and Darsena II. We docked at Darsena II.

The trip up the channel and the docking were normal. After we docked, the captain called for a meeting of all deck and engineering officers in the salon, with only the duty engineer excused from attending.

When everyone was assembled, he started to talk. It was very much a proclamation.

"This childish nonsense between all of you and Sparky will cease immediately. There will be no discussion, no protestations of innocence, nothing. If anything like this ever happens again, I will personally see to it that each and every one of you lose your license. Dismissed!"

With that, he walked out of the salon, leaving us all stunned.

Roy was the first to break the silence with his classic "Sheeeit!"

Before he could follow it up, the chief engineer turned to him, pointed his finger and said, "Can it! Not another fuckin' word! You got it? In case there is anyone here that doesn't know, someone trussed Sparky up like a turkey and hung him upside down in his cabin. He hung there for over an hour. The purser tells me that he thinks he may have burst some blood vessels in his eyes, and he is nauseous and dizzy. No matter what anybody may think of Sparky, that's carrying this shit too goddamn far! Is that clear, Roy?"

Roy just looked at his feet and didn't answer.

"I said, is that clear, Roy?"

Still not meeting his stare, Roy muttered, "Yeah, Chief. It's clear."

The mate said, "Well, I guess this meeting's over. Go on about your business."

Roy followed the chief out of the salon and stopped him just outside the door to his room.

"I know you think I did this, and to tell ya the truth, if I'd thought of it, I probably would have. But, Bill, I swear, it wasn't me!"

The chief stared at him for a few seconds and said, "Roy, it's hard for me to swallow this one."

"Jesus, Chief, I admit I hate the asshole. But I didn't do it! Did he say I did?"

"The captain said Sparky didn't know. He said someone came into his cabin while he was at the radio console, pulled a bag over his head, yanked him out of his chair, and trussed him up. He's pretty sure it was more than one person, but he doesn't know who."

Other than the excitement with Sparky, Monte was pretty much a blur. We stayed for a day and a half, and I never got ashore. The only part of Montevideo that I got to see was the cranes and the roofs of the sheds along the pier. The mate told me there wasn't much there that wasn't also in Buenos Aires and that the people in Buenos Aires were a lot friendlier.

After dropping the pilot, the captain decided he didn't want to run all the way back to the end of the channel and the outer buoy. He decided to shorten the trip around the shoal area Banco Ingles by some forty miles by swinging the inner buoy and continuously making course adjustments. We rode the thirty-foot sounding line until we were due south of a buoy marking a wreck. We then settled onto 295 degrees and ran that line until we intersected the channel leading into Canal Intermedio. There aren't any other captains I knew who had the balls to do that. It's akin to surfboarding in shallow water with a 484-foot ship.

Chapter 19

BUENOS AIRES

We dragged our feet on the river since it is only an eight-hour run between ports. The local pilot was picked up at the pilot station about five miles prior to the Buenos Aires main approach channel where Canal Sur split off and continued on Canal Norte into the North Harbor and the docks.

The mate was right about the people; they were very friendly. The racetrack impressed me the most. I only went to the track once back at home, and it was kind of seedy and populated with blue-collar workers. Of course I had never been to the clubhouse, only in the stands. A lot of folks I knew were avid bettors, either on the dogs at Wonderland or the ponies at Suffolk Downs, but I had neither the money nor the inclination. The track in Buenos Aires gave me an insight into how the rich folks lived: elegant and classy.

The next most impressive thing was the beef. Incredible! You could get a prime rib or filet mignon dinner at a classy restaurant for about three dollars. The same thing in Boston would have cost at least twenty dollars. The beef was so good that the officers all chipped in and bought two hundred pounds of filet mignon at fifty cents a pound so we could barbecue whenever we didn't like what was on the menu on the return trip north. Filet mignon is good, but by the time we reached the Caribbean, we tired of filet. I ground some up for hamburgers and seasoned them heavily just for a change of pace.

I took a tour bus around the city with an English-speaking guide. BA is a big city!

In Rio, I had gotten a taste of the difference in Latin lifestyle, particularly the timing of the workday and mealtimes. It was even more different in Buenos Aires. No one ate dinner until at least 2200 hours. It took getting used to.

At 2130 hours, Greg, Tony, the mate and chief, Roy, and I all went out to dinner at a fancy restaurant called Amigos de El Toro. This was my first exposure to what they called the Birthday Club. The regulars on the ship had a round robin of nights out. Depending on whose birthday was next on the list, that person had to treat all the others. In the course of a year, it all evened out. Tonight, it was the mate Dennis's turn to treat. He explained the rules of the game to Tony and me.

"The chief keeps the official list of birthdays and whoever is next on the list is host for the night. The host pays for everything, and I do mean everything, from the foot of the gangway until we return to the gangway unless one of the group goes off and does his own thing. The minute someone leaves the group, the host is off the hook for the rest of the night. You can even get laid and have the host pay for it, but you've got to get laid in the presence of all. That's usually what breaks up the party. A smart host will take everyone to a cathouse, hoping someone gets horny enough to leave."

The restaurant was old-fashioned elegant. Blazers and ties were our uniform of the night, and we were severely underdressed. The men in the crowd wore business suits or tuxedos, and the women mostly wore gowns, with a smattering of dinner dresses. We opted to be seated on the patio. I think the staff was relieved since we wouldn't be too close to their obviously elite clientele.

Starting with a glass of champagne, each of us offered a toast to the mate. Everyone took a shot at criticizing the recipient and also tried to upstage the previous toast. It was definitely more in line with a roast than a toast. I didn't know enough about the mate to offer any insightful remarks and didn't have the nerve to take a cheap-shot insult, so I played it straight with, "May this birthday not break your bank account." At least he smiled when I toasted him.

At 0100, we finished our cognac and cigars and piled into two taxis with Roy leading the way. True to form, we ended up at a first-class whorehouse with no sign on the door. Instead, there were business cards depicting a silhouette of a nude, voluptuous woman, a telephone number and the words "Avec Plaisir." By then, I was more than a little drunk. It didn't even dawn on me until the next day that it was ironic that the joint had a French name until I realized that although no one there spoke French, most of them practiced it.

Suddenly standing up and shouting, "Aw sheeeit!" Roy grabbed one of the girls and headed for the back. The mate was officially released from his host obligations. Tony was the next to go, and I ended up flipping a coin with the mate to decide who would get a spunky little bundle of energy named Mayda. He lost.

The next morning, the mate asked, "How was Mayda?"

"May-da my night," I replied, and his response was a blank stare, obviously not recognizing, much less appreciating, my attempt at humor.

"She lived up to her billing. She had lots of energy—a lot more than I did!"

Chuckling, he walked away.

After four days, we finally buttoned up the hatches and cast off. As far south as we were going to get, halfway through the trip, we were heading north again.

Chapter 20

FIRE AT SEA

All during the trip, there was an uneasy truce between the second mate and me. I think that he appreciated the fact that I would keep his charts organized and updated without making a big deal of it. But for my part, I couldn't stand him because he was such a slob. No one had yet seen him take a shower. He also had the disgusting habit of pissing into his sink at night rather than walking to the head at the end of the companionway. That didn't improve the already fetid odor in the room. On more than one occasion, the mate had pointedly remarked there were some strange odors on the mates' deck, and he suspected that maybe some mice had died there. The mate also mentioned to me one day that the second's room needed fumigating and maybe they should smoke the room with an aerosol.

Half a day out from port at 0335 hours. In my quest to conquer the dictionary and vastly improve my vocabulary, I was up to *flirtatious*. It's funny, but as much as I hated grammar school and being taught by nuns, the lessons they pounded into me stuck. Sister Mary Beatta taught us that if you want to learn a word, say it aloud three times, spell it aloud three times, and write it in a sentence three times. Do that, and you will own that word forever.

As usual, Sister Beatta was right, and I marched my way through the dictionary during my boring sea watches. When I got to a word I didn't know, I would do the drill and thus garner another bit of ammo for my verbal arsenal. My grammar skills were practically nonexistent, but I had a feel or sense of what was right by either just looking at a word on paper or taking a mental snapshot. I couldn't tell you why it worked, but when I put a sentence together, it was right 99 percent of the time.

As I said, I was finishing *flirtatious* for the third time when my nose interrupted my concentration by detecting the smell of smoke. Just seconds later, the ordinary came running onto the bridge shouting, "There's smoke coming from the second's room!"

I immediately thought, "Jeez, the mate's done it! He's smoking him out!" But I nixed that idea because I figured it was way too much effort for the mate to get up at that time of night.

"Go wake up the captain!" I yelled as I bolted out the door and down the ladder to the mate's deck.

As I turned the corner, the companionway was already thick with smoke pouring out from under the second mate's door. I tried the knob, but it was locked. Turning, I banged on the chief mate's door and yelled for him to get up. Going to both port and starboard watertight doors, I hooked them back so the smoke could clear out.

When the mate came stumbling out of his room, I told him to get the key to the second's room because it was locked. He turned and grabbed what I assumed was a master key from his desk and stood there holding it. Seemingly wide awake, he wasn't very responsive. Just then, the fire alarm went off, and the mate simultaneously broke into a fit of coughing. I grabbed the key, fumbled it into the lock, and turned it. Remembering my firefighting training, I dropped to my knees and pushed slowly against the door. It cracked an inch or two, but something was blocking it. The smoke and heat hit me in the face, blinding and choking me. I was about to back away when someone grabbed me by the belt and yanked me backward. It was the mate. He pulled the door shut and said, "Don't open it until I get a hose."

"I can't! There's something blocking it."

Smoke continued to billow out from under the door, and it seemed to be getting thicker. The captain arrived just as the mate did with the hose and the bosun. I didn't think anything of it at the time, but it later struck me as odd that someone as tuned in to the goings-on aboard his ship as the captain hadn't been there sooner.

The captain and mate looked at each other for just an instant, sending some sort of signal between them that I could sense but not read. Then the mate yelled, "Hit it!"

The ordinary, who had been standing at the hose station, turned on the water.

The mate yelled to me and the bosun, "Open the door and duck!"

I shoved hard, and the door slowly opened. The next thing I felt was spray as the mate pushed by me into the room with the hose.

It only took about a minute to put out the fire. It was the second mate's body that had been blocking the door. He lay there, a naked, partially seared blob of flesh. All I could think was, "A cannibal barbecue!" A macabre thought, but other than witnessing a shooting when I was a kid, it was the first up-close death I had seen, and it really threw me. Apparently, he had been trying to get out of the room when he was overcome. He was slightly scorched on his right side where the mattress had started to burn, but it appeared it was the smoke that killed him. Either that or he had a heart attack from the stress. Given how obese he was, either was possible. The mate checked for a pulse but there wasn't any.

The captain came in, gave a low whistle, and ordered me to return to the bridge. As I left, I heard him tell the mate, "Get a body bag from the purser and put him in it. On second thought, double up on the bag. Make room in the meat locker, and put him in there. We'll put him ashore in Paranaguá."

On the bridge, coughing and wheezing continuously, I did a quick course check, did a horizon check from both bridge wings, and then stood on the starboard wing and started shaking. I had had fire training with the Boston Fire Department as part of our safety training. Part of it was to surround you by a ring of fire with only a small extinguisher in your hand. Another time we had to get out of a burning, very smoky building without a gas mask. Both times were mainly training to avoid getting panicked. Seeing the second mate's body added a dimension of reality.

I'm not sure how long I stood there—probably not more than a few minutes. I felt a hand on my shoulder, startling me. I turned. The captain was standing there.

"It's pretty gruesome if you've never seen anything like that before."

"Yeah, it was!"

"You okay, sonny?"

"Yes, sir. I'm all right."

In fact, I felt giddy, like I wanted to laugh but knew I shouldn't. It was pretty bizarre.

"Finish the second's watch. Come and see me in my cabin after Mr. Adams relieves you."

"Aye, aye, Captain."

After he left, I did another horizon check and walked back into the bridge. By this time, the AB from the four-to-eight had the wheel, and he asked me what had happened.

"It looks like the second fell asleep smoking and burned himself up."

He didn't press me any further.

Walking back out to the starboard wing, I lit a cigarette and resumed my shaking. After the first puff, I shuddered, recollecting that it was probably a cigarette that killed the second mate. Immediately, I stubbed it out and flicked it overboard. I went the entire watch without a cigarette.

At dawn, I shot some stars and fixed our position at 113 miles south of the pilot station.

Tony relieved me at 0730 hours. He was early because he wanted to find out what had happened. Incredibly, he slept through all the noise, including the fire alarm, which I thought was an impossibility. The only ones on that deck I hadn't actually seen during the ruckus were Tony and Sparky, though I wasn't surprised at Sparky's nonappearance because he had been avoiding all of us like the plague ever since the hanging incident. After relating the experience to Tony, I went down to get breakfast.

As I walked in the officers' salon the captain waved me over to his table.

"Sonny, that was a nasty mess last night. You handled things pretty well."

"Thank you, Captain."

"Now that the shouting is over, please write a detailed report of the entire incident, sign and date it, and turn it in to the mate."

"Aye, aye, Captain."

"Make sure you note that his door was locked when you first got there."

"Aye, aye, Captain," I responded, but immediately thought, "How odd! Why would he want that mentioned, and how would he know? The door was unlocked before he arrived at the scene."

"That's all."

"Aye, aye, Captain."

I turned and left, too wound up to even eat breakfast. I took a shower but was too rattled to sleep, so I got a writing pad and pen, went down to the officers' salon, poured myself a coffee, and started writing the report.

Every minute, I'd stop and think, "How did the captain know the door was locked, and why is it so important?" By the time I finished, I still didn't have the answer. But the adrenaline rush had slowed, and weariness had taken over, so I just hit the sack and conked out.

I slept for only a couple of hours before the mate called us out for docking in Paranaguá.

Chapter 21

REFLECTIONS

Sitting in his cabin, trying to make sense of the entire incident, the captain reflected and once again asked himself, "Why did I ever promise Seymour? I should have just waffled and never made a commitment."

The Seymour he referred to was his older brother, who, until the day he died, had been the captain's personal hero, someone he had always admired and respected.

Even now, twenty years later, the captain could hear his voice as clear as if his brother were standing next to him. He still felt the pressure on his hand from his brother's viselike grip when Seymour asked him to look out for his only son as he lay in the hospital bed the day before his surgery.

"You never know what can happen when they put you under the knife," Seymour had said. "I've never asked you to do anything before for me," which, sadly enough, was true. "But I'm asking now. Promise me you'll watch out for Dorothy and Sam if anything happens to me."

"Nothing will happen to you, you'll see. You'll be right as rain in a few days."

"Promise me! I need to hear you say it!"

"I promise, Seymour. I promise."

"Good. Dorothy is the finest woman I ever met. I still don't know why she married me, but I've been grateful she did ever since. Why she put up with the likes of me all these years I'll never know."

"Seymour, you ought to give yourself some credit. After all, the fact that you took on the burden of her child when you married her is no small thing."

"A small price to pay for all the happiness she's given me."

"Tell me, Seymour: Why didn't Dorothy let you officially adopt Sam?"

Averting his eyes and speaking softer, Seymour replied, "I tried to talk her into it after we'd been married a couple of years, but she didn't even want to discuss it. Finally, after I persisted, she said, 'You've done enough taking him into your home and helping raise him, but he doesn't deserve your name. I love Sam dearly, but I want him to know there is a world of difference between the good man you are and the no-good son of a bitch who abandoned me when I was eight months along. I want Sam to keep his father's name so he'll know that is all that he ever gave him, and a name means nothing unless the bearer of the name has character and integrity. Sam Grossman was a coward who ran away from his responsibilities. I don't want his son to romanticize him or be like him.'"

The next morning, less than thirty minutes after they wheeled Seymour into the operating room, the doctor came out and told Dorothy and the captain that Seymour had died. Apparently, he had an embolism that burst in his brain, and he died within minutes. Dorothy died ten years later.

Now, as he sat there, the captain thought, "Thank God neither Seymour nor Dorothy can see Sam now. Apparently, he was just like his father: lazy, shiftless, and unreliable. Oh well. I made a promise, and I did my best to live up to it."

He tried to piece together what the mate and bosun had told him about the broken lock and the burned section of floor. It was clear that the fire wasn't caused by any cigarette. Some sort of flammable liquid had spilled on the floor. It had either started on the floor and flared up the side of the bunk or vice versa. He also knew it was unlikely that Sam had started it. As a boy Sam had once burned himself on the leg, such that he had a very real fear of fire. He only used safety matches and never used a lighter for fear of lighter fluid. He smoked a lot but never smoked lying down. The captain also knew, as did everyone else on board, that Sam never locked his door. Yet it was definitely locked.

Initially, he thought the reason Sam never locked the door was because the deadbolt on the inside was broken. But the bosun told him that the paint scratches on the door around the lock were too deep, actually scratching the metal as well, to be caused by fingernails. Besides, Sam constantly chewed his fingernails. There wasn't anything in the area that he could have made the scratches with, so it would seem they were made by someone else. The only obvious conclusion was that someone had set the fire, broken the lock, and locked him in the room from the outside. The question was, who?

On the deck above, sitting in front of his console, tuned out to the immediate world but listening in on the ether, Sparky was pondering as well.

Now that things had calmed down and the initial shock was wearing off, he congratulated himself on pulling it off. He never meant for the pig to die. He just wanted to get even with him and scare him for hanging him upside down. Sparky knew that the hanging prank was the second engineer's idea and that he was mainly responsible. But when they picked him up, the unmistakable odor of that pig filled the room, and when they grabbed him, he could feel the sheer bulk of the guy. There was only one person that big who smelled that bad.

Sparky mentally admired his own handiwork. Getting the key off the second mate's key ring was easy. The second never carried the ring with him except when the ship was in port because that was the only time the bridge got locked. Everybody thought Sparky was tuned out to them when he was at the console, but he was very alert to the sounds and happenings of the ship around him. It was a trait he had developed over the years, something those moronic idiots could never have done, especially the second engineer and that pig, the second mate.

Entering the second mate's room at 0500 hours when the second was on watch, he grabbed the key, took the lock apart, went back to his room, and ground down the deadbolt latch using his modeling grinder, knowing that the second never locked his door and wouldn't notice. He then went back and replaced the lock. He had already concocted his miniature Molotov cocktail using the paper cup and woven threads for a fuse. By inserting the threads into the side of the cup near the bottom using a suture needle he had taken from the steward's medical kit, he fixed it so the lighter fluid would seep out onto the thread and there'd be just enough heat to burn the paper and cause the lighter fluid to flash.

What really pleased him was the fact that he had summoned up the nerve to creep back into the second's room when he was asleep. At that time of night, the only ones awake were the men on watch, and none of them came onto the officers' deck except to call out the next watch. He placed the mini-Molotov on the edge of the bunk, lit the thread, and still managed to close and lock the door quietly from the outside. He got back to his room well before there was any commotion.

"It was too bad the pig had to die, but at least he won't be bothering me anymore! Now all I have to do is figure out a way to get even with that other idiot, the second engineer."

Sparky never noticed the key to the second mate's room still sitting on the edge of his desk near the bunk.

Chapter 22

PARANAGUÁ

When we docked, the usual cotillion of customs and immigration officials paraded on board, along with the local ship's agent. The agent told us that the local authorities had refused permission to take the second's body ashore. We would have to keep him on ice, literally, until we reached Rio.

That evening after supper, I walked by the second's room, and the bosun was standing in the doorway, working on the lock.

"What's up, Boats?" I asked.

"I'm replacing the lock."

"What's wrong with it?"

"The deadbolt latch was ground off. I thought maybe the second panicked and tried to turn it the wrong way trying to get the door open, and it snapped. But when you look at it close, you can see it was ground down. Without that, you can't turn the lock except with a key from the outside. Kinda weird."

Leaning in, I said, "Can I look?"

"Go ahead. Maybe your young eyes are better than mine."

Stepping into the room, I looked around at the floor and quickly realized there wasn't any place for the broken piece to have gone. The perimeter of the room was solid except for directly under the little desk, and I could see that space clearly as well. There wasn't any broken part there, so it didn't just break off. It must have been ground down, just like Boats had said.

Looking at the door, I noticed there were scratches on the paint around the lock.

"Did you need pliers to unscrew the lock barrel?"

"No. I have a special wrench that keys into the perimeter slots. Why?" I showed him the scratches, and he said, "Yeah, I saw those."

Then he stopped and just stared at me.

"What's wrong?"

"I'm the only guy on board who works on locks. It's a hobby I picked up. I haven't ever changed this lock, and all the doors and bulkheads were painted just before you all came aboard in the shipyard. I wonder if the second made these trying to get out."

We both shivered at the thought of Sam clawing at the door.

"By the way, Boats, is there a master key for all the mates' and engineers' rooms?"

"Yeah. I got it."

"Is that the only one?"

"No. The mate has one too. Why?"

"Just curious."

The next morning, the mate asked me to witness the listing of Sam's personal gear. The mate had gone through the drawers and closet and laid out all his stuff on the now bare bunk frame. As we went through the list, I ticked off two small key rings. One had a key to the bridge and the chart room, and the other had a key to the case for his sextant—a Plath, a good one—a luggage key, and one other key that looked to be a key to a train station or airport locker. Other than the number, there was no way to tell what it belonged to.

"I don't see his room key anywhere."

"I don't either. It must have got lost in the mess."

I told him about what had transpired with Boats changing the lock, and he responded, "I better tell the captain. That's unusual."

Knocking on Sparky's door, the captain didn't wait for a response and entered in his usual imperious manner. Sparky was seated at his desk, and the captain perched on the edge of the bunk next to it.

Sparky was antsier than usual, twitching, shifting in his chair, refusing to meet the captain's stare.

"What's wrong, Sparky? You seem agitated."

"I'm okay."

"I was wondering if the second mate had sent any out messages recently," the captain asked.

Sparky reacted like he had been hit with a cattle prod.

"No. Nothing," he stammered, keeping his eyes on the deck.

It was then that the captain noticed the room key on the edge of the desk, and he instinctively palmed it. Sparky was too busy studying the floor tiles to notice.

The captain got up and left without another word.

In his cabin, the captain fingered the room key, wondering why he had grabbed it. Suddenly, he felt the hair on his neck rise. Calling for the bosun, he asked him if he still had the old lock to the second mate's room.

"It's in the trash can in his room."

"Please get it for me, Boats."

"Aye, aye, Captain." He left the cabin, returning with the damaged lock parts.

"Would you please reassemble it for me?"

"Aye, aye," he replied.

In less than a minute, he had the lock back together.

"Thank you, Boats. That will be all."

After the bosun left, the captain inserted the key into the lock. It turned.

"Tit for tat, Sparky. Tit for tat."

Chapter 23

RIO NORTHBOUND

It was only a nineteen-hour run at our normal sea speed, so we had to slow down in order to arrive at the pilot station at 0600 hours. The captain still avoided anchoring. He seemed to consider having to do so as a black mark against him. This time we hit a rare opening in the schedule when there wasn't another ship waiting to enter the harbor. Normally, we would try to beat out other ships to be first to arrive at the pilot station and thus be first to get into port. All this was subject to some baksheesh—a bribe—but most of that took place between the local agent and the pilot association. Normally they told us to either hurry or slow down.

With the second mate gone, the captain had set six-hour night watches for Tony and me, and the day watches stayed the same. The chief mate would relieve us for breakfast and dinner from 0600 to 0800 and 1600 to 1800 hours. It wasn't too bad, though I hoped it wouldn't be this way all the way home. The overtime was great, but it made for a long day.

As the pilot boarded, he informed the captain that there would be an ambulance at the pier for the body of the second mate, and the local police would also be there. He said the crew was to stay on board until the police completed their investigation.

The investigation turned out to be four bottles of scotch, ten cartons of Marlboros, and a half hour of bullshitting in the captain's cabin, during which they asked only three questions:

"What was the second's name?"
"Were there any witnesses?"
"What were their names?"

Even though it was coldhearted, it seemed weirdly appropriate for a man named Grossman, who was such a social misfit, to be treated so cavalierly in death.

Playing tourist on this visit, I went to Corcovado and enjoyed the magnificent view from the top of Sugarloaf. Tempted as I was to head for Ipanema and see if I might run into Claudia, I decided not to, since my last departure was rather ignominious. I left well enough alone.

Chapter 24

RECIFE

Arrival at Recife was on Thursday, August 4, at 0400 hours, and we killed time circling the ship off the pilot station. Most times they wouldn't bring the ship into port before 0600 hours.

Coming up the coast, we approached on a bearing of forty-three degrees until we picked up the flashing green buoy at Banco Ituba and then adjusted to ten degrees to ensure we were close enough to the next buoy at Banco Victor Pisani. When that buoy was abeam to port, we adjusted to 312 degrees until we had the flashing red sea buoy on our starboard beam. Making a lazy turn to port into Canal Olinda to line up with the approach to the breakwater, we waited for the pilot to board.

Recife is a small port, nothing exceptional about it. Attached to the northeast shoulder of Brazil, it was generally the last stop before heading home, except every third or fourth trip they'd call at Belém on inducement.

Expecting to be here two days, the mate broke sea watches just after docking at 0700 hours. I had the day watch, so it was the usual routine of watching the longshoremen sweat their asses off manhandling the cargo, in this case bags of quebracho, and keeping them from getting into the crew quarters to steal anything.

Quebracho is some sort of extract from a tree bark. I'm not sure, but I think they use it in the tanning of hides. The smell isn't too bad, but it's filthy, dusty stuff and has the consistency of molasses-colored concrete. It looks like they pour it into the jute bags, and it must harden, because it's misshapen and hurts like hell if you drop it on your foot. My view standing up on deck watching was a lot better than in that hold throwing those bags in the heat.

Tony relieved me, and I made a beeline for the shower. Just climbing down the hatches once an hour, I was filthy from the dust. After a hard day in the heat, I was ready for a shower. Roy had told me about a joint called the Moulin Rouge, named after the famous Paris bistro, although he also said this place had nothing in common with the original except bare tits all over the place. Roy and I headed there for some R&R.

In an area where all the surrounding buildings were no more than two stories, this one stood five stories tall and looked like a hotel. Walking in, we were hit by a wall of noise and a cloud of cheap cigarette smoke, both of which made me flinch. An enormous, battle-scarred bar ran the full length of the left-hand wall. The rest of the room was filled with tables, chairs, and noisy, smelly bodies. The males were obvious customers and ran the gamut of the United Nations. The ladies were, well, not ladies.

Roy proceeded to explain to me that the place was set up on different tiers of business, and he took me on a showcase tour.

The first floor consisted of a bar, live—sort of—music, and no-touch B-girls. The second floor was set up like a café, and the booze was served to the tables. The music was an old jukebox guarded by the ugliest, meanest-looking human I had ever set eyes on. He didn't speak, just sort of grunted and glared, but he sure did communicate. You could look at the selection, all in English, even some local songs, but touching the jukebox was taboo. To get music, you handed Senor Mean-and-Ugly some money, told him the letter and number of the song you wanted, and he would punch the number in. Took me a few times to figure out that it didn't make any difference how much money you gave him. As long as it was more than one cruzeiro, he would play the song once. Also here on the second floor were some touching-allowed B-girls.

The third floor was, for all intents and purposes, a "get ready to get laid" room where the hookers strutted their stuff. The hookers still tried to hustle you for drinks, but their main purpose was sex. This is where all the tit-flopping, crotch-grabbing, stink-finger stuff went on in preparation for the hardcore finale.

The fourth floor—I never did get to see the fifth floor—was one large room. There were bathrooms with no doors at one end and a central corridor lined on both sides with iron rods suspended from the ceiling by wires. The rods were draped with curtains that formed dozens of little cubicles, with a bed in each cubicle. It was truly a flesh factory.

A hooker would take a john to one of the cubicles and have him take off his pants, including shorts if he wore them. Shirt and shoes were optional. Then she would take him by the cock and lead him, elephant style, to the bathroom with no doors, where she would wash the guy's cock and balls before taking him back to the cubicle and fucking him. The experienced johns were the ones who carried their wallets in their hand when they were out for their elephant walk.

"Roy," I said, "this is a little too much for me. I'm going to stick with the first floor and just drink a lot."

Laughing, he replied, "Yeah, I think you're right. This place gets raunchier every time I come here."

We went back down the stairs to the noise and smoke.

Shouting to be heard, I yelled, "Cuba libra and cerveza!"

The bartender smiled and nodded, so I presumed he had actually heard me. Lighting up a smoke, I looked for Roy and saw him talking to a guy down the bar. Roy waved me over and yelled, "William, my boy, meet Bernie. Bernie sails with Cunard Line. We met in this same bar about five years ago and drank ourselves unconscious."

Bernie reached out, shook my hand, and yelled, "What say we give it another go, eh?"

Looking past me, he waved at the bartender, who walked our drinks down to us and set them on the bar.

"Bottoms up!" he cried, and Roy and I chugalugged our drinks. Bad start!

Within an hour, we had tossed off six drinks, and there was no doubt that I was the rookie in the bunch.

I thought, "I should slow down and pace myself."

That was my last cogent thought of the night. Then I pretty much stopped thinking.

Pain! Deep, throbbing pain. The kind that is both an ache and a stab all at once. Mostly in my head, but as consciousness grew, lesser aches in my back and legs began to surface.

Smell as well! A pungent, earthy, sweaty, body kind of smell mixed with farm odors. Not the fresh-cut-hay type but more like chicken shit heaped on cow manure.

Both eyes were shut, but there was brightness in my left eye, and I wondered what was wrong with my right eye, but I just couldn't connect the dots. Finally, I opened my eyes a crack. As the sunlight stabbed me, the pain level went through the roof, so I slammed them shut. I swear I heard them slam.

Inching to my right, I opened them again and saw the offending ray of sun, but it had missed me this time by about six inches. It seemed to be coming through a tiny hole in what I took to be the roof. Staring at the ray of sun, something beside me, a large something, moved. Turning toward it, I strained to see. It looked at me, and groaned, thinking "Oh shit! What the fuck did I do now?"

Lying beside me on a filthy straw mat was a fat, ugly, nearly toothless woman who was grinning vacantly at me. We both were as naked as the proverbial jaybird. Her black and my pasty white made us look like outsized piano keys. Mine looked stained due to the tan lines on my arms.

My first thought was, "Please, God, I hope I was too drunk to fuck her!" The rest of my thoughts were less worthy of consideration.

Managing to sit up, I realized I was sitting on a grass mat on a dirt floor in a hut made of sticks and with a roof of tin and boards. I got to my hands and knees, felt bilious, crawled to the doorway, and threw up on what would have been a front stoop if there were one. Stumbling to my feet, I looked back at the woman. She seemed to be passed out.

After my eyes had adjusted again to the semigloom, I spied my clothes in a heap on the floor, managed to discern, barely, arms from legs and which end goes on what first, and I slunk out of the hut, a picture of abject misery.

Though I was striving desperately to recall how I got there, absolutely nothing came to me beyond that sixth drink at the bar with Roy and Bernie. A total blank!

I gave that up and concentrated on figuring out where I was. It was then that I realized I was in the middle of the jungle. Now, fear began to mingle with the rest of my anxiety. I didn't panic, but I didn't avoid it by much. Finally, my navigation instincts and training took over. It was obviously morning. If I was in the jungle, the sun, hence the ocean and the port, had to be to the east, since everything else was to the west of the port. All I had to do was head east until I hit the ocean and then figure out if I had to go north or south to reach the port.

As I was conducting this brilliant strategy, I realized I was standing at the edge of a road. It wasn't much of a road as roads go, but it was definitely a road. Wonder of wonders, it seemed to go in an east-west direction, so I started walking east. Follow the sun.

I had stumbled along for about half an hour when I heard engine noises coming up behind me. It turned out to be a bus—a rickety, smoke-billowing, noisy, gorgeous bus—and I waved it down. The driver gave me a long, hard look before he opened the door. When he did, I asked, "Recife?" and he nodded.

Climbing on, I started to take a seat when I heard, "*Senor! Cinque cruzeiros!*"

Of course, he had to say it about three times before it sunk in that he was demanding bus fare. In that instant, I realized I had not even checked my clothes for my wallet. Miracle of miracles, it was there, and so was all my money. I had to add honesty to the descriptive adjectives of last night's sleeping partner. I gave him a twenty-cruzeiro note, and despite my protests, he insisted on giving me change. All in all, my impersonation of an ugly American was working perfectly.

We reached the city about an hour later, never once seeming to go faster than fifteen miles per hour, with multiple stops as we got closer, including a piss break for the driver. We arrived at a bus station in the center of town. From there, I was able to get a cab back to the port.

As I climbed up the gangway, Tony stood at the top, pointedly stared at his watch, and greeted me scornfully with, "Right on time to relieve me, I see."

It was 1100 hours, and I was supposed to relieve him at 0800 hours.

"Go hit the sack. I'll take it until 1600, but you owe me big time."

"Thanks, Tony," was all I could manage.

I fumbled my way to my room, puked one more time, and passed out.

BELÉM

This was an interesting approach since we made it in the dark. Afterward, the captain said that most captains wouldn't run this stretch of river in the dark, but he wasn't "most captains." I wasn't sure if he was just bragging or not, but I do know the landmarks and buoys were not easy to sight. I was a nervous wreck because of all the shoal areas that were shown on the chart but weren't clearly marked by buoys.

We were on course 246 degrees, and it was getting tight as we squeezed between Banco do Clemente to port and the unnamed shoal inside Banco São João to starboard. We picked up the three-second flashing light at Pta. Taipu and then picked up the ten-second flasher. When that bore 157 degrees, we altered course to port to 226 degrees and ran for about ten miles. When that same light bore 108 degrees, we altered to port again to 189 degrees and ran for another five miles. Finally, we tracked a two-second flasher marking the shoal off Ilha do Quati. When that bore 156 degrees, we changed course to starboard to 232 degrees and ran that to the Belém approaches.

During this time, we had been pumping ballast to get the bow down so the ship was trimmed as flat as we could get it. The draft in the port of Belém was only fifteen feet, and we were right at the limit. Considering that we were only going to pick up about two hundred tons of cargo, I couldn't figure out why we bothered, but the captain said it had something to do with the line "showing the flag" there rather than any real commercial interest.

When we reached the northern apex of the naval anchorage, we were creeping along at five knots trying not to churn up too much river bottom, and we altered course to 184 degrees. Once we cleared the southern edge of the naval anchorage, we changed course again to 197 degrees and then followed the channel line into the berth. The channel was only about five hundred feet wide at its narrowest points. With the tug alongside, we took up half the width.

There was no doubt whatsoever that this place is where they put the Vaseline on the nozzle before starting the surgical procedure of inserting the enema into Brazil. Just up from this anal orifice on the Amazon River, anything beyond Belém was pure colon and intestine, no place you would go on a pleasure cruise.

At 1600 hours on Wednesday, we inched our way off the berth until we got to where the channel opened up wide enough to turn the ship. The captain was mumbling to himself, "They should pay us for dredging their damn channel," but not loud enough so the pilot could hear him. After turning, we crept back through the pier area and finally got past the naval anchorage into enough water so the captain dared to take a deep breath and headed downriver.

Chapter 26

LAST NIGHT OUT

Tonight was the last night for me as grill chef. We had taken turns cooking on a charcoal grill we had set up beside the pool on the passenger deck. We had bought filet mignon in Buenos Aires, and no one wanted it skillet fried, which was the only way the chief cook knew how to cook meat, ergo volunteer grill chefs. All the meat was cooked to order, and all the officers, including the mate, took their turns cooking.

About four days ago, we had ground the filet into hamburger just for variety's sake, and this was the last of it. The timing was perfect since we would hit Jacksonville sometime the next night.

I actually enjoyed cooking on the grill. Concocting a special barbecue sauce that I made up on the spur of the moment, I told everyone it was a secret recipe handed down from my grandfather on my father's side. It made for good conversation, but in reality, to my knowledge, my grandfather never barbecued anything except his fingertips when he burned himself lighting his pipe. Everyone except the chief cook liked it, so I cooked his without any sauce. He never actually said he liked my cooking, but he always cleaned his plate. There were never any leftovers. Agreeing to let him partake of the filet mignon became essential because he supplied everything else. Besides, he halfheartedly threatened to report it to his union business agent if we didn't cut him in on the deal.

Sitting in the salon poking at the remnants of an apple pie, I asked the mate whether he thought the captain was going to give Tony and me a good recommendation.

He looked at me a few seconds absent-mindedly. Then, seeming to collect himself, he said, "Actually, I think he will. He likes both you boys."

"I hope I'll be able to keep this third's job when we hit New York. I'd like to go back and revisit some of those ports, especially Rio."

"Well, unless something strange happens, you should have no trouble keeping the job. Neither should Tony. The last I heard from Marine Ops, they were having a tough time filling all the billets. So long as Vietnam keeps up, I expect the job situation will stay strong. A lot of the trampers are chartered out to MSTS."

My inquiring look prompted him to continue. "Military Sealift Transportation Services provides the ocean transportation needs for the Department of Defense. Come to think of it, the name has just recently changed to Military Sealift Command—MSC. The crews on those ships are getting war-zone pay, plus the differential for carrying ammo and bombs. That's where the old timers are going. We're getting all the school-ship guys like you."

"Did you get war-zone pay when you were running there?"

"Yeah, but to tell you the truth, I felt kind of guilty about it. Some of the others did too. We weren't in any area where anything could happen to us, and most of us have friends or relatives that are over there getting their asses shot off on army pay."

He paused, seemingly reflecting, then continued, "A bunch of us contributed our war-zone pay to the USO. It just didn't seem right to keep it. In any case, you won't be seeing Rio anytime soon if you stay on board, because we're getting shuffled again. They're finally putting the old girl into the trade she was built for: the Great Lakes. We're going into the lakes and then down to Africa."

"Wow! Where in Africa?"

"The same run that Robin Line runs, south and east Africa up to Mozambique."

As I left the salon and headed up the ladderway for the bridge, I heard Sparky's shrill voice screaming, "Get out of my cabin! You don't scare me! You think you're so fuckin' smart, pulling all those stunts and embarrassing me. Well, I'll have the last laugh when I tell the brass in New York what you and the others have been up to. I know what you've been doing! I'll see that you lose your ticket and never sail again! Now get out!" The next thing I heard was a door slamming.

When I reached the top, I looked and saw the back of Roy, the second engineer, stepping out of the back door onto the deck. He didn't see me, but he really slammed the heavy WT door, no easy feat, so he must have been really pissed off.

Walking into the bridge, I nearly bumped into the captain, who was leaving. "Sparky got a little loud there, eh, sonny? Were you the target?"

"No, captain. He was yelling at the second engineer."

"Well, guess I can't blame him for that."

And he walked out.

We blew through Jacksonville, Savannah, and Baltimore on the way north. Because we were filling in a gap on the schedule, all the loading in South America had been lighter than usual. With the ship changing routes again—switching over to the African run—we wouldn't be doing any loading until we were southbound.

Chapter 27

SAVANNAH

L ying in his bunk, Dennis, the chief mate, had been tossing and turning all night, unable to sleep. He hadn't had a good night's sleep since the day before arrival at Jacksonville, knowing he would be running the gauntlet for the rest of the trip up the coast. Short runs between ports and having to call out the entire deck crew for docking and undocking and long days loading and unloading didn't leave much time for sleep.

"Sweet mother of Jesus," he thought. "I'll have a fuckin' ulcer before this trip is over."

They were safely docked in Savannah, and the longshoremen were due to start at 0800 hours. It was a little after 0300 hours, so he got up, went out on deck, and lit up a cigarette.

Walking aft, he saw Roy and another guy, a stranger, talking in the offshore passageway of the deck locker. They shook hands, and Roy reached down and handed him a bag. The stranger walked aft around the fantail and headed for the gangway. The mate recognized the burlap sack Roy had removed from the coaming the night they dumped the beer and sewing machines overboard and immediately thought, "The son of a bitch is selling some of the shit on his own," and called out, "Roy!"

The guy on the gangway was startled, slipped on the top step, and lost his balance. When he tried to grab the railing, he let go of the bag, and it fell to the pier below, spilling its contents.

"Jesus, Mate, what the hell you doing?" Roy yelped.

As he was talking, the mate came down the ladder and headed for the gangway, hot on the heels of the stranger, Roy following close behind.

The guy was picking up what looked to be bricks and stuffing them back into the bag when the mate reached the bottom. Picking one up, Dennis read the printing and blanched. It was C-4, the American version of Semtex.

Turning to Roy, he rasped, "Are you out of your fuckin' mind? Where'd you get this stuff? Who the fuck is this guy anyway?"

Instead of answering, Roy said, "Hey, man, put that away. You don't need it. He's a friend."

Turning, the mate saw the stranger had a Colt .45, old-time army issue pointed at him, and he just stared at him, dumbstruck.

Roy said again, "I told you. He's a friend. Pick up the rest of the stuff and just leave. No problems."

"Back off," the guy said.

Focusing, the mate willed his legs to move. Roy did the same. They just stood there until the stranger finished picking up the bricks. Backing away, he said, "Go back up the gangway, and don't look back."

That's exactly what they did.

At the top, the mate looked over his shoulder and saw that the guy was already at the head of the pier in full flight.

"What?" was all Dennis said to Roy.

"Not here. Let's go to your cabin, and I'll explain."

The first thing the mate did when they reached his cabin was take a piss. He was shaking so bad, it was a wonder he hadn't pissed all over himself.

"So, explain!"

"I got the stuff from a guy in a Seabees outfit. They blow up a lot of things over there, and no one would miss it."

"Why?"

"I just wanted to have some explosives. He needed some cash, so I paid him a hundred bucks, threw in ten cases of beer, and paid for a hooker that worked in the bar where we met to give him a blow job. I was just gonna take it home and maybe blow something up back in the hills. But when we were forced to dump the sewing machines and beer, I figured I might not get another chance to get it. So I took it out and stashed it."

"Where?"

"In the stack housing, up high in the steel framework."

"Jesus! It's bad enough that you stuck a bag of explosives in where we had to weld the plate. What if a spark or hot metal had hit it? Now you're telling me that you put it in another hot spot to hide it. The fuckin' thing might have cooked off and taken the whole ship apart!"

"No way! You can't set it off by burning it. It has to be detonated."

"How do you know that?

"The Seabee guy told me."

"Christ, Roy, I thought you had some common sense. The fuckin' guy would have told ya you could eat it like candy if he thought he was getting money from ya! So who was the guy that just scared the shit outta me?"

"Just a good old boy I knew. I called him from Jacksonville, and he was interested in buying it, so I sold it all to him. I got an extra thousand bucks for the detonators."

"What? You mean you kept the detonators in the same bag as the C-4? You fuckin' idiot! Get out! Get the fuck outta here before I lose it and throw you the fuck overboard!"

After Roy left, Dennis got the shakes again, felt his stomach roiling, went into the head, and puked.

"Un-fuckin'-believable!" he thought and reached for a cigarette.

Roy didn't come into the salon for breakfast, and his absence was conspicuous, since he never missed a meal. Even the captain commented.

"Where's our Dixieland emissary today?"

No one responded, and that was the end of it.

Right after breakfast, as the supervisor for the longshoremen was leaving the mate's office, the chief engineer stopped in and asked, "What's going on, Dennis? I just saw Roy. When I asked him why he missed breakfast, he said, 'The mate and I had some words, and I'm giving him a wide berth for a while.' What gives?"

Signaling him in, Dennis shut the door and explained everything that had happened.

"Do you think he was trying to sell any of the guns too without us knowing it?"

"That was my first thought last night, but I think he's telling the truth. He was hustling the C-4 on the side. The stupid shit could have got us all killed."

"Just let him stew for a while, Dennis. He ought to sweat for a few days for being such a horse's ass!"

Chapter 28

ENGINE PROBLEMS

We dropped the pilot off at the pilot station and cranked up to sea speed. Around 0200 hours, there was what sounded like an explosion in the engine room. A bunch of alarms went off at once. I called the captain, but before the second ring, he walked onto the bridge.

"What's the situation?" he asked.

"I don't know, Captain. I heard a big bang, the smoke and fire detector went off, and the revolutions are down to about fifty and dropping fast."

"Have you called the engine room?"

"No, sir, I just got off the phone from calling you."

"Well, call them."

"Aye, aye, Captain."

Turning to the phone, I called the engine room, but no one picked up. I immediately called the chief engineer's room. There was no answer there either.

"No one's responding, Captain."

"I have the con. Go down to the engine room, track down the chief, and have him call me ASAP."

"Aye, aye."

"And, sonny?"

"Yes, Captain?"

"Be careful. Don't walk into a shit storm down there."

"Yes, sir."

I bolted down the interior passageway to the main deck and slowly cracked the WT door leading into the engine room, expecting to see a lot of smoke. Instead of smoke, it was thick with steam, and I could hear the roaring of live steam somewhere down below, which made me even more nervous. I could be walking into a steam-line break and never know until I stepped into it. Live steam will cut you cleaner than the sharpest sword. Closing the door again, I retrieved a fire axe from the fire station on the bulkhead. Entering the engine room, I reversed the axe, holding it by the blade and waved it in front of me like a blind person with a cane. The only difference was that I moved it vertically as well as horizontally. If it was a live steam leak, it would take out the handle of the axe before getting me. I might get burned, but at least I wouldn't get sliced by high-pressure steam.

Descending the ladder was like being in a steam room, except a lot noisier. Feeling my way along, I found no one at the main control board, so I kept going down to the fireman's level. There I found the chief and the first engineer.

"What are you doing here?" the chief yelled at me.

"The captain told me to find out what's going on. No one answered the phone," I shouted back.

"We had a blowout! Something hit the return line to the condenser and ruptured it. We're shutting everything down. Tell the captain that we can't give him any power to the engines until we know what happened. We've already started the auxiliary generators for electricity, so he can use the anchor windlass if he has to. But we can't turn the prop until we fix the problem."

"The captain wants you to call him."

"The phone is close to the rupture point. Just go tell him what I told ya."

I turned and made my way back up the ladders, moving a little faster now that I knew a scythe of live steam wasn't waiting in ambush for me. Putting the axe back in its station in the companionway outside the engine room door, I ran to the bridge and told the captain the news.

"I've ordered the bosun to ready the anchor. When we lose headway, I'll drop it." Pausing, he scratched his chin and then said, "Go find Sparky and tell him to send an alert to the coast guard."

Grabbing my arm, he continued, "Not a mayday, you understand, just an alert. When he's done that, tell him to come see me, and I'll have a message for him for vessel operations."

"Aye, aye, Captain," I replied and took off for the radio room.

When I instructed Sparky on what to do, he started to ask a lot of questions. I shut him up by telling him the captain wanted me to let him know the instant the message was sent.

I returned to the bridge, and the captain sent me right back to Sparky with a request to amend the message to the coast guard by giving them our exact position, which he had written down for me and let them know we would drift until we could determine the extent of the damage. I trotted back to the radio room and passed it on.

"Sonny!" the captain called out. "Keep the bosun on the bow. I'll drift for now, but I want him ready to drop anchor on short notice. Have the helmsman go up to the flying bridge as lookout. Bring the ordinary up, and have him stand by with you on the bridge as an additional lookout. I just checked the radar, and there isn't any ship traffic right now, just small stuff. But I want you to keep it on long range and check the screen every five minutes."

"Aye, aye, Captain."

That was how the rest of my watch went.

At 0700 hours, the chief reported to the captain that the repairs were made. They had cut out the broken segment of return pipe and welded a new piece in its place. They had no way of pressure testing it but deemed it safe to crank things up again. At 0715 hours, we secured the anchor and proceeded to New York. The captain insisted that we not go to extra nozzles for sea speed, and we cruised along at seventeen knots all the way to New York.

At breakfast with the chief, I asked him what caused it.

"It's the damndest thing," he said. "Those pipes are built to take a hell of a lot of pressure, but it didn't take much to snap it from shearing."

"What caused it to shear?"

"The weld broke on the overhead frame that supports the chainfall we use for repairs whenever we have to lift the head off the condenser. That big chainfall came down right on top of the pipe. It must have hit the pipe right on its edge, because it sheared that pipe as clean as if a knife had cut it. The damndest thing I ever saw. The odds of something like that happening are out of sight!"

He was still mumbling to himself when I walked out.

Chapter 29

BROOKLYN

New York, while still strange territory to me, was no longer part of a different planet. Still, I was hoping I might get a chance to get home to Southie if we were in port over the weekend.

Discharging operations started at 1300 hours. The mate had Tony and me on day work since the union hall would be sending night mates. Around 1030 hours, the ship boss, the same one who worked the ship when we were there last, came up and said, "Hey, Mate, you got a minute? There's someone who wants to meet you."

"Who's that?"

"A friend of mine. He's down in his car at the head of the pier."

"I'm on duty. I can't leave the ship."

"I asked the mate, and he said it was okay."

"Let me check with him. I'll be right back."

"Sure."

The mate was in his office, and I told him about the ship boss's request.

"It's okay to go, but don't take anything, you understand?"

"What do you mean, don't take anything? What are you talking about?"

"The guy you're gonna meet is the son of the longshoreman that had the heart attack when we were in last. He wants to personally thank you for what you did for his father."

"Oh. Is that all? Well, he doesn't have to do that."

"He thinks he does, so just go along with it. Remember, don't take anything if he offers. By the way, he's one of the local Mafia capos, so remember to be polite."

Back on deck, the ship boss was waiting for me at the top of the gangway. "The mate clue you in?"

"Yeah, but this really isn't necessary. I would have helped anyone that was in that situation."

"Yeah, well, good for you, but that wasn't just anyone, it was Frankie's father, so he has to show his appreciation."

As we neared the car, a big, black, four-door Buick loaded with chrome, two men got out, one from the driver's seat and one from the rear. The guy from the rear leaned in and said something, and another guy got out. Standing about five foot ten, he was trim but with exceptionally big shoulders. Wearing a gray sports jacket and tan slacks, he seemed friendly until I saw his eyes. They were cold, icy. I didn't quite shudder, but I thought about it. Stepping toward me, he smiled with his lips only, held out his hand, and said, "Hi, William. I'm Frankie. I wanted to thank you personally for saving my father's life on the ship."

"Nice to meet you, Frankie. I appreciate you going to all this trouble, but it isn't necessary. I was just doing my job. I'd have done it for anyone."

The smile disappeared. "It was special to me. I just wanted you to know that I owe you for what you did for my father. If there's anything you need, anything at all, just get in touch with Ritchie here," he said, pointing at the ship boss, "and it'll get taken care of."

Noticing the absence of his smile, now I was nervous. "Thank you very much, but I really don't need anything. I'm glad I was able to help your father, and I hope he's doing okay."

The smile façade returned. "Pop will be fine, thanks to you. Just remember, anything at all, see Ritchie."

Reaching out, he shook my hand again and climbed back into the car.

As the car drove away, Ritchie said to me, "You look like you're gonna puke. You okay?"

Grinning sheepishly, I wisecracked, "I've never been in the presence of royalty before. I guess it made me a little nervous."

"Royalty!" he roared. "That's a good one!"

He slapped me on the back so hard my neck almost snapped.

As we walked back to the ship, he said, "Frankie means it, you know. If you need anything, you got it. You go anywhere or do anything in Brooklyn, it's on the house. You need a TV, refrigerator, car, you name it, you got it!"

"Thanks. I appreciate it. I am curious though. Given the 'influence' that Frankie has, why does his father still work as a longshoreman?"

"His old man is stubborn. This is where his pals work and spend their time, and that's where he is going to be. Frankie gave up trying to talk him into other stuff a long time ago."

As I climbed the gangway, Ritchie, staying on the pier, called out one last time, "Anything at all, understand?"

I just smiled and waved.

Back on board, I tracked down the mate and related what had happened.

"All I can say is, I'd rather have them liking me than disliking me." Looking me in the eyes, he said, "Still wouldn't be too smart to take anything though. If you do, Frankie might begin to feel that you now owed him. Besides, whatever you got would probably be hot anyway."

At 1230 hours, the mate said, "I'm going up to the bar just outside the gate and get some fried oysters. Wanna come along? My treat."

"Who's gonna watch the store?"

"Tony can handle it. I already asked him, and he doesn't like oysters. He made that clear."

"What do you mean?"

"He called them fish snot, either fried or raw."

"That's pretty descriptive, but I'll go. Let me go wash up."

Hustling to my room, I took a leak, washed my face and hands, and then hotfooted it down the gangway, catching up with the mate at the head of the pier. As we passed the guard shack and started to cross the street, I saw the same car that Frankie, the capo, had been in when I met him. On the sidewalk side, leaning into the rear window, was a small guy. When we reached the other side of the street, he pulled away from the window, turned away from us, and started walking down the street. It was Sparky.

Grabbing the mate's arm, I said, "Hey, look! That's Sparky!"

"So?" he said.

"He was just talking to Frankie. You know, the Mafia guy. At least he was talking to someone in Frankie's car. What would a weasel like that have to do with Frankie?"

"Fucked if I know," he said, and we continued on to the bar.

Circumstances prevented me from getting home to Southie. We sailed on Saturday at 2200 hours. The weather was clear, and it should have been uneventful. It was anything but. In retrospect, I think everyone was tired and not as sharp as they should have been. The subsequent investigation cleared everyone of negligence, but my conscience still bothered me, wondering if I could have prevented it somehow.

As we were backing out of the berth at Twenty-Third Street, we fed the tug at the stern a lead through the after starboard chock and tied it off on the bit. We were using the new nylon mooring lines, but only to the dock. For the tugs we used the older poly lines. For whatever reason, Pickerel, my number two AB, passed the nylon line to the tug, and neither I nor Sturm, his partner, noticed it.

To compound matters, when he threw the turns on the bit, he flipped the second turn like you do the top and last turn. When the tug took the strain, the line on the bit immediately bound up so that we couldn't easily let it loose. It happened fast, but it looked like slow motion. Sturm yelled to Pickerel to slack off, but for some inexplicable reason, Pickerel stepped to the rail and started to wave at the tug. I guess he was trying to signal it to back down. Just then, the nylon, stretched past its limit, snapped right at the bitt. It came at Pickerel like a scythe and cut off both of his legs right at the knees. I don't think he even knew what hit him.

I froze for about two or three seconds. Then I leaped past the bitt and pulled Pickerel away from the rail. Blood was everywhere. Stripping off my belt, I yelled to Sturm to give me his belt too. I used them both as tourniquets high up on each thigh. I stuck my utility knife under one belt and Sturm's fid under the other belt to put more pressure on Pickerel's femoral artery. It was then that I realized that the captain was talking to me on the radio. I cut him off and told him Pickerel had lost his legs and I needed bandages immediately. At the same time, I told Sturm to take the OS and lower the gangway so we could carry Pickerel down to the tugboat on a stretcher. That would be the fastest way to get him ashore.

All the while I was doing this, Pickerel was moaning, incoherent and obviously going into serious shock. He was trying to sit up and kept clutching at my arm. "You've gotta stay lying down," I kept telling him. At the same time, I stripped off my shirt and T-shirt and tried to wrap them around the stumps. It didn't really accomplish anything insofar as stopping the bleeding, but I didn't know what else to do.

Just then, the chief steward arrived with his medical kit and a box of Kotex. It was the perfect dressing for the ends of the stumps. He checked the tourniquets, told me not to touch them, and went back to swaddling the stumps. Just as he got out the morphine to give Pickerel a shot, Sturm and Goode, the OS, came running up with the Stokes litter basket, a stretcher for emergencies. The steward gave him the shot, and we lifted him into the litter and dog-trotted to the gangway, with the steward right behind us.

As the tug approached the pier, I could hear the scream of approaching sirens. The ambulance, along with four fire engines, was waiting for us at the end of the pier. They wouldn't let any of us go with him in the ambulance. As it pulled away, the head of vessel operations, a guy whose face I recognized but whose name I couldn't remember, told us to all get back on the tug, so it could take us to the ship, which was going to anchor. That's what we did. Not a word was spoken on the trip out.

When we got aboard, the mate told us to go clean up and then report to the captain. It was then that I realized that the steward and I were both covered in blood.

Before going up to see the captain, I walked back aft to look at the scene. The line had had enough force left after taking off Pickerel's legs to bust through a section of the railing as well.

For a sissy, the steward showed a lot of guts and poise, coolly stepping in the way he did. Maybe I needed to do another reassessment of my personal assessment capabilities.

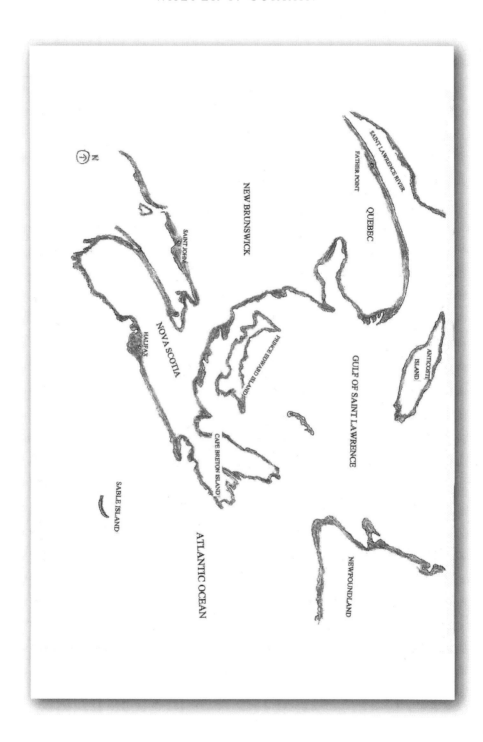

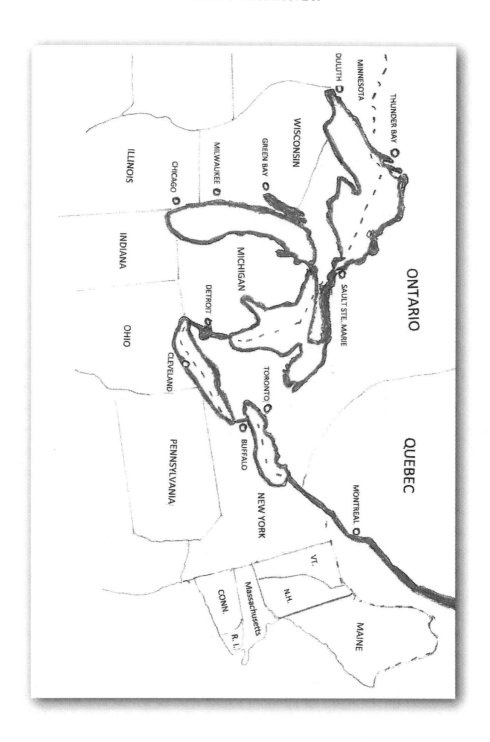

Chapter 30

PASSAGE TO MONTREAL

We finally got clearance to sail at 0600 hours. After we dropped the pilot, we spun ship to verify variation. Every ship has both a gyrocompass and a magnetic compass. Gyrocompasses always read true north, and magnetic compasses read magnetic north. Since information on maps and charts is always related to true north, magnetic differences have to be accounted for. Spinning ship, or "swinging the compass," is a process whereby the ship is turned in a full 360-degree circle while taking readings on a fixed object whose position is known. By matching the readings of the gyrocompass to the magnetic compass, we can tell the differences in bearing, called variation, also declination. That is recorded, and if we have to use the magnetic compass, we can make the proper adjustments to our course. Also, since magnetic compasses are affected by their surroundings, each compass has to be adjusted to offset that magnetic interference. That is called deviation. On a typical ship, the magnetic compass has two iron balls, one on each side. The deviation can be adjusted by sliding the balls closer to or farther from the compass. These balls are traditionally referred to as "the captain's balls."

After spinning ship, we set course for Sable Island. Sable Island is a crescent-shaped island approximately 110 miles southeast of Halifax, Nova Scotia.

In that area known as the Graveyard of the Atlantic, there have been more than 350 shipwrecks recorded since 1583. Five people live there year round, and some tourists go there in the summer. It is where you make the turn north between Nova Scotia and Newfoundland. From there, we'd round the Gaspé Peninsula and pick up the Saint Lawrence River pilot at Father Point.

We sailed from New York without the loran-C working. Loran-C was developed during World War II, but even in the 1960s, it was the latest navigation system, using hyperbolic radio signals at low frequencies from a number of different stations, each with a slightly different frequency. With a range of 1,500 miles, the accuracy was within ten miles. Special charts showing the lines of the radio signals allowed the navigator to plot a position by reading the closest intersecting point of two signals. Without the loran-C we weren't quite flying blind; there were always sun and star lines to rely on. But at sea, on overcast days without landmark references, you were guessing at your position. About twenty-four hours out of New York, we lost our gyro compass and had to rely on the magnetic compass. Right after we changed course off of Sable Island, heading in for Cape Breton, fog set in. It was pretty thick, but the captain didn't slow down any. The radar picked up a lot of small boat traffic and few ships. Abeam of the east end of Cape Breton on a due north heading, we lost the radar. That's also when we noticed the magnetic compass was occasionally drifting as much as ten degrees, first east, then west. None of this was good news. Other than our radio direction finder, we now were using the same essential tools that Columbus used five hundred years earlier.

When the radar failed, the captain told the engine room to shut down the extra nozzles and take her down off sea speed so that we could slow down in a hurry. But he still maintained eighteen knots. We were flying blind.

The captain plotted the course by dead reckoning, and we managed to get one good fix with the radio direction finder as we approached the tip of the Gaspé Peninsula, with Anticosti Island off to the east.

Slowing down to five knots, he had the bosun break out the sounding lead. Grabbing a walkie-talkie, the captain told me to get one and keep it handy and then went below to join the bosun at the rail. From just forward of the amidships passageway, the bosun tossed the lead and got a sounding. I was on the bridge wing looking down at them, and I saw the captain feel the tallow on the bottom of the lead and actually taste it. He then looked at what seemed to be a small chart he was holding.

"He thinks he's Captain Ahab. No one can tell where they are by doing that," I thought.

Looking up to the bridge wing, he ordered me to alter course to port eight degrees, which I did.

Fifteen minutes later, he repeated the process. This time, he changed course three degrees to starboard.

For the next three hours, he repeated this but other than looking at the small chart he held in his hand, he never came up to the bridge to check a chart. Every second or third time, he'd make a course adjustment. Finally, he came back to the bridge, ordered engines to slow ahead, called out the mate to stand by the anchor, and had the bosun rig the pilot's ladder on the starboard side. He then got on the radio and called for the pilot station. When they responded, he gave them our estimated position, explained that we had no radar, only a magnetic compass, and requested they send a pilot aboard. Less than twenty minutes later, much to my astonishment, the pilot boat pulled alongside, and the pilot came aboard. The captain had just taken us clear around the Gaspé Peninsula in conditions that were reminiscent of the old days of sailing ships, and he had hit the mark exactly. The old adage "wooden ships and iron men" came to mind. Later on, even the mate said that he was impressed. He said, "I have always respected the captain's seamanship ability. I don't know if the captain really could tell from seeing the type of bottom and tasting it, or if he was putting on an elaborate show, but he did an outstanding job of dead reckoning. Either way, it was the goddamndest piece of seamanship I've ever seen." I told him about the small chart the captain had looked at. "I have no idea what that could be." He said.

The pilot wouldn't proceed upriver in the fog without the radar. Unlike in the open ocean, he had shoals and narrow waterways to contend with, so we followed the pilot boat to the anchorage about a mile away and dropped anchor to await clear weather.

Chapter 31

TRANSITING
MAD DASH

Even though we were not scheduled for any cargo activities in Montreal, we had to stop and have all of our nonfunctioning equipment repaired. That took two days due to scheduling issues with the radar repairman.

The Great Lakes Saint Lawrence Seaway System is a complicated and fascinating gateway to the Great Lakes, the greatest inland waterway in the world. Extending from the Saint Lawrence River to the western end of Lake Superior, it is 370 miles long, but the critical portion consists of six fairly short canals containing a series of locks, with a total length of only about sixty miles. The Canadians operate five of the seven locks from Montreal to Lake Ontario, and the Americans operate the remaining two. The Canadians operate all eight of the Welland Canal locks and the Iroquois Canal lock. The Americans operate all four of the Saint Mary's Falls Canal locks. The difference in elevation from one end of the system to the other is about 590 feet, and the entire system is gravity fed.

To navigate a five-hundred-foot-long ship can be hair raising due to the narrowness of the channel in places and the fact that ships pass within five feet of each other. Starting at the port of Montreal, you enter the South Shore

Canal, starting with Saint Lambert and Côte Sainte Catherine Locks. That is fourteen nautical miles. Then there is the Beauharnois Canal with its two locks for a stretch of thirteen miles. That links Lake Saint Louis to Lake Saint Francis. Next is the Wiley–Dondero Canal, which has two US-controlled locks, the Snell and Eisenhower Locks, for an eight-mile stretch. After that is the Iroquois Canal, which has only one lock. That is only about 0.3 nautical miles long and opens into Lake Ontario. All the time you are traveling in a roughly southwest direction.

After transiting Lake Ontario, you reach the Welland Canal, which takes you from Lake Ontario into Lake Erie. There are eight locks, and they are numbered, not named. Seven of them are at the north end, and one is at the south end. Three of the northern locks are twinned and contiguous, but the others are single-passage only. The eighth lock at the city of Halifax (not Nova Scotia) is a control lock just above Niagara Falls and is the entrance to Lake Erie. Going east is equally as arduous even though you are traveling downstream.

Unlike the Panama Canal, where the mini–railway engines called "mules" tow you through the locks, every ship has to navigate on its own using its own mooring lines and engines. We had a small man-boom rigged over the side with a bosun's chair, and we lowered a couple of crew members to the dock at every lock to be our mooring line handlers. We picked them up the same way after letting the last line go in each lock. It got pretty tight at times, especially at the approaches to the locks, where it got very narrow. When we passed some of the lake ore boats, both ships had to "go to the bank" and rebound off the bank suction to maneuver around one another. It was old hat to the lake crews, but a little nerve-wracking to us saltwater guys. Even the captain was a little tense at times, although he had been there before.

Farther up the lakes is the last canal, Saint Mary's Falls Canal. This links Lake Huron to Lake Superior. It has four parallel locks at Sault Sainte Marie.

The locks were simply a series of "steps" that were interconnected. Open the front gate, slide in, close the gate behind us, let the water from the higher lock (or river) flow in, open the new front gate, and move out. When we got to the next lock, we repeated the process.

It was fascinating to stand on deck and watch the ship rise in the lock, like watching the tide come in but at a much faster pace. It's nature at work with just a little help from man's ingenuity. I could hear the gurgling of the water, but it was muted, as if from a far-off waterfall.

One of the more memorable occasions happened when we transited the Welland Canal on our inbound leg. There was a tourist viewing platform right at the edge of lock number three. When we were inbound on the low side and started to rise, we were treated to a great view looking up the skirts of half a dozen women on the platform waving at us. Naturally, we smiled and waved back. It wasn't until one of the ABs called out to the bosun, "Boats, look at all that snatch!" that the ladies caught on, grabbed their skirts, and stepped back from the railing. All except one, a small blonde who actually put her foot up on the railing, giving us a completely unobstructed view of her pink panties. For that, she got a standing ovation and a lot of whistles.

This was a marathon sprint. From the time we let go the last line at Montreal, we raced through the lakes. Toronto, Buffalo, Cleveland, Detroit, Duluth, Green Bay, Kenosha, Racine, Chicago, and then a straight shot back to Montreal. Because of our speed of twenty-one and a half knots, we set speed records between some ports. We would arrive at port in the morning, work all day until 1100 hours, work all day the second day, and then sail that evening and race all night to the next port, where we would do it all over again.

The strangest place was Kenosha. We loaded KDs—disassembled autos referred to as "knocked downs" in crates—from the auto plant in Kenosha. They actually called high school kids out of classes to work when the ships came in. The stevedores were regulars, but there wasn't enough steady work to support a large workforce. Instead, they used the kids to work as longshoremen.

At Green Bay I managed to con the mate into letting me go off at noon to get one drink at Paul Hornung's bar. I wasn't a Packers fan, but every football fan had heard of Hornung's bar, so I felt obliged to go. One drink only; I was working.

The Detroit River was filthy, and the traffic was incredible. That was another place where ship and barge traffic was tighter than a gnat's ass.

In the twenty days we were on the lakes, I never got more than three hours' sleep in a night. The mate never broke sea watches, and Tony, the other third mate and I worked cargo watches as well. It was great for the money because we made a small fortune in overtime. But I was happy to leave the lakes behind.

September 20 and it was snowing like a son of a bitch! A regular whiteout. Really a snow squall, it hit just as we were entering Saint Catherine's Lock on the final leg of the lakes. Normally, if there isn't any backed-up ship traffic, it takes about forty-five minutes to transit a lock. When the squall hit us, we already had the nose of the ship into the lock, so there was no stopping. It was so bad we couldn't see the pier when we lowered the two men down to handle the mooring lines. Relying heavily on their shouting, we made sure we didn't dump them into the lock. The captain refused to move out until the squall started to abate. Over the radio, the traffic controller was squawking and obviously didn't like the delay, but the pilot whispered to the captain in a heavy French accent, "No problem. It's your ship, not his." There wasn't anything the traffic controller could do about it. After about an hour and fifteen minutes, we inched our way out of the lock and into the channel. By the time we had transited the Saint Lambert Locks and passed the piers at Montreal, it was down to just a few flurries. We had no trouble down the river, dropping the pilot off at Father Point and heading out to sea.

Chapter 32

HEAVY WEATHER

Clearing Cape Breton, we ran into the remains of Tropical Storm Greta. The captain wanted to stay inside Sable Island to stay out of the northeast quadrant of the storm. Not too large in area, the storm wasn't much as far as tropical storms go, but the seas were running about thirty-five to forty feet, and we were getting bounced around pretty good.

Most people who have never been to sea associate rough weather only with getting seasick, but that isn't all. In really heavy seas, you end up getting black and blue on your elbows, forearms, hips, and shoulders, mainly from banging into bulkheads and doors as you move around the ship.

We were on a heading of 225 degrees, and the seas were generally on the port quarter, so we were doing a lot of corkscrewing. I was out on the port bridge wing and had left the slider door open leading into the bridge. As I turned and headed back inside, the ship rolled to port. Just as I reached the door, I felt a shudder and was struck in the back by green water. It drove me into the bridge, and my foot caught on the door coaming. Going down hard on the deck of the bridge, I smashed my chin and damn near knocked myself out. As the ship rolled back to starboard, I continued to roll all the way across and ended up in a heap against the starboard-side door, which, luckily, was closed.

Struggling to my feet, I managed to get back to the port side and shut the door. But there was still about six inches of water in the bridge that was slowly draining out the after door leading down to the captain's deck.

Goode, the ordinary, was on the helm, and he asked me if I was all right.

"I think so," I replied. "What the hell happened?"

"Musta caught a freak wave. I thought the side ports were gonna blow out."

I picked up the phone to call the captain. Just then, he walked in through the after door. Expecting all hell to break loose because I had been dumb enough to leave the door open, I was amazed at how calm he was.

"Well?" he queried.

I explained what happened, and his only comment, after hearing me out, was, "You won't do that again, will you, sonny?"

"No, sir!"

Walking to the port side, he stared out for about a minute. Then he said, "That's the second time I've encountered a rogue wave. I didn't like it the other time either." Turning to me, he said, "Get the electrician up here to check and see if anything has shorted out. You better patch up your chin too."

And he went below. It was then I realized that the front of my shirt was soaked with blood. The point of my chin had a jagged tear in it from my encounter with the deck. I wadded up my handkerchief and pressed it to my chin.

I called the chief engineer and asked him to send the electrician to the bridge, relating what happened. He repeated what I already knew, "Mother Nature is a mother."

Breaking out the first aid kit, I went into the pilot's room and gave myself five stitches to hold my chin together. I had a lot of training in suturing at school, using raw chicken breasts for practice. After daubing antiseptic on it, I taped a gauze pad over it and returned to the bridge.

When I got there, the electrician was finishing his inspection, and he told me everything seemed okay. He would check the passageway on the way down to see if any of the runoff had gotten into anything. I thanked him, and he left. When I reported to the captain that nothing was damaged, he asked what I had done to fix my chin. I told him, and he seemed impressed by my suturing skills, stating, "Let's hope you don't need to use them any more on this trip."

Later, after I had been relieved by Tony, I calculated that the wave must have been sixty to seventy feet high. On an even keel, the eye level at the bridge wing is fifty-four feet above the water. Even with the roll to port, for a solid sea to come over the top of the wing, it would need to be at least sixty feet high.

Chapter 33

BROOKLYN REVISITED

As soon as we docked, the company safety director came aboard and questioned me, Strum, and the chief steward about Pickerel's accident. Pickerel was alive, but it had been touch and go for the first few days. The director seemed satisfied with our answers and left the ship.

In the morning the mate told me to keep an eye on number three hatch. We would be loading special cargo, mostly cigarettes, into the lockers in the tween deck, and a mate had to be on site at all times. There were legendary stories of ingenious ways the longshoremen could steal cigarettes and liquor right under the noses of the watchmen, and I was a little nervous.

In Boston, while working as a "scalawag"—what they called nonunion dockworkers, as opposed to "cleanheads" and other names in other ports—I listened to the mates on the ship lament about all the cartons of scotch with wet stains on the bottom. But not one case was opened, so there was no shortage. They checked the longshoremen as they came out of the hatch. No one was carrying anything except the water bucket. What the mates didn't see was the longshoremen removing the lid of the water bucket, wrapping cheesecloth across the top of it to act as a strainer, then smashing the case of scotch against the bulkhead and letting the scotch drain through the cheesecloth into the water bucket.

As I said, I was a little nervous now that I was on the other end of the situation.

When I came out on deck, the first person I saw was the ship boss, Ritchie. "How ya doin', Mate?"

"Fine, Ritchie. How have you been?"

"I'm good. Anything I can do for ya?" he said with a knowing look.

Pausing, I replied, "As a matter of fact, there is. I like working for this company, and I'm trying to make a name for myself. Today, for instance, I'm going to be working special cargo in number three hatch. You know how the company leans on the mates to make sure damages and losses are kept down. Well, if you could sort of pass the word that the men take special care whenever I'm on duty, it would make me look good, and it doesn't cost anyone anything. Make that happen, and I'd be grateful, and I sure wouldn't need any more favors. What do you say? Think that could be arranged?"

Staring hard at me, he slowly grinned and said, "You're smarter than I thought, Mate. Let me talk to the guys and tell them to be extra careful when they're working with you."

"Thanks, Ritchie," I said, shaking his hand. "I really appreciate it."

Not one cigarette or can of beer was missing when we finished the specials. The mate said he'd never seen a completely clean loading of specials before. When I told him about the deal I made with Ritchie, he laughed like hell!

That night, for whatever reason, we didn't have any night gangs ordered, so most everyone took advantage and took the night off to go uptown. Having not been paid yet, I was short of cash, since the last cash draw I got from the purser was in Recife, so I decided to stay aboard. Around 2130 hours, I went up to the flying bridge to have a cigarette. I liked it up there because there were a couple of lounge chairs by the pool, and it wasn't too cold, so I could sit and relax. The ship could carry up to twelve passengers, but there were none on this trip, so the pool area was my private smoking lounge. Finished with my smoke, I stubbed out the butt and walked back into the bridge to take the inside ladderway. As I passed Sparky's cabin, I heard him talking to someone.

Thinking it was strange because Sparky hardly ever spoke to anyone, I tried to eavesdrop.

"It's happening right now! You gotta hurry and get here!"

That was all I heard. Then it sounded like he was moving toward the door, so I hurried around the corner of the passageway and went all the way around and out the inboard door to the deck.

I glanced over the side as I was making my way back and saw a large utility truck parked by the gangway. At first I thought it was ship's stores being delivered. As I watched, though, I saw the mate and the chief engineer carrying long boxes down the gangway and putting them into the back of the truck. Immediately I forgot about Sparky. There were three other guys I didn't recognize helping them. From what I had seen before, I just knew that this wasn't legitimate. Being a city boy, my first instinct was to turn away and go deaf, dumb, and blind. It doesn't pay to get involved in stuff that's none of your business.

I knew this must be the remains of what had been in the coaming at number three hatch, but I hadn't seen them get it out, so they must have been pretty careful.

Still watching, I saw one of the strangers hand a large envelope to the mate, pat him on the shoulder, get in the truck, and drive up the pier. When they were past the bow of the ship, I walked down below toward my cabin and literally bumped into the mate as I stepped out of the ladderway door onto our deck. Both reacting like we had been shot, we leaped back from one another.

"What are you doing here?" he asked.

"I didn't see nothing!" was my response. The instant I said it, I realized how stupid it sounded.

"Come into my room," he ordered.

Now I was more than a little apprehensive. Putting the mailer envelope he was still carrying on his desk, he sat down and said, "Now just what is it that you didn't see?"

"What?"

"That's not an answer."

"What?" I repeated, knowing full well I was in deep shit.

Before he got to ask again, we heard sirens from out on the pier. He got up and walked out to the corridor, walked inboard, through the door, and looked over the side. Not knowing what else to do, I followed him. Down at the foot of the gangway, there were two US Customs cars and three city police cars. About a dozen uniforms were running toward and up the gangway.

"Shit!" he mouthed, then turned to me and said, "Get in your room and stay there. Remember, you know nothing!"

By this time, I was more concerned about the customs and cops than I was about him. I went straight to my room and locked the door. It had barely clicked shut when there was a lot of shouting out in the corridor. I heard the mate's voice and the captain's voice, then the noise subsided.

After about fifteen minutes, there was a knock at my door. I ignored it at first, but when a voice said, "This is US Customs. Open the door!" I walked over and opened it, doing my best to look as if I had just woken up.

"Come with me!" the customs agent said and ushered me into the captain's day room.

Along with me, jammed into the room were the captain, mate, chief, second engineer, purser, three customs agents, and two of New York's finest.

The older of the customs agents seemed to be in charge. He asked me who I was.

"I'm William Connolly. I'm the third mate."

"Have you been aboard the ship all day?"

"Yessir."

"Where have you been for the last couple of hours?"

"In my room."

"Why didn't you answer when Agent Cummings knocked on your door?"

"I did answer. I must have fallen asleep. When I heard the knocking, I got up and opened the door."

"Have you seen anyone that isn't a member of the crew on board the ship?"

I thought a minute and then answered, "Yes."

As I answered, I glanced at the mate, and he looked positively ashen.

"There were a whole bunch of longshoremen aboard most of the day, and the ship chandler was here around noon."

"I meant in the last two hours," he barked.

"Oh. No. I was in my room all the time."

He fixed me with a hard glare for about ten seconds. Turning to the captain, he said, "No one in this room leaves the ship without my permission. Understand?"

The captain, looking very calm and nonplussed, replied, "Of course, Inspector. You all heard the man, gentlemen. No one goes ashore until we get this matter all cleared up."

"No one goes ashore, period, until I tell them they can!" the agent barked out again.

The captain merely nodded and waved his cigarette in that imperious manner of his.

The mate started for the door, so I turned and walked out in front of him. I headed down the ladderway to our deck, with the mate right on my heels. I was hoping I could avoid him. But when we reached the deck, he whispered, "Come with me," and led me into his day room.

"You better stick to your story. Understand?"

I just nodded.

Turning toward his desk, he muttered, "Oh shit," under his breath and then said, "Wait!" just as I was leaving. Taking the envelope from the desk, he handed it to me and said, "Put this up in Sparky's cabin. He's gone ashore, but I have the key."

Before I could think, I blurted out, "No, he isn't. He's up there. I heard him talking to someone."

He stared at me.

"How could you hear him talking to someone?"

I didn't answer. I just stood there looking trapped.

"Never mind, wait here," he said and stepped into his bedroom.

When he came out a few minutes later, he had a bundled-up shirt in his hand, and it was obvious there was something wrapped in the shirt. He took the shirt and, turning his back to me, shoved it into a chart tube. He then wrote out a mailing label and stuck it on the tube. Handing it to me, he said, "Bring this to the purser, and tell him to put it with today's mail. Go on. Get out of here. By the way, you better stick to your 'I was in my cabin for two hours' story."

When I dropped the chart tube off with the purser, I saw that it was addressed to the mate at an address I presumed was his home address. There was no return address. If it got lost in the mail, it would stay lost.

Returning to my room, I spent the rest of the night trying in vain to sleep.

"Are any of the cops still here?" the chief engineer asked the mate as he walked in the door.

"Not that I know of, but you better be looking over your shoulder from now on."

"What the hell happened?"

"Near as I can tell, the customs guys got an anonymous tip that something was being smuggled ashore from the ship. They called in the locals, and that's when all the noise started."

"Are they onto anything?"

"Not that I can figure. The guy I talked to thinks it was a drug deal and some of the crew is involved. So far, unless they're leading me down the path, they don't suspect any of the officers. They did ask a lot of questions about the second mate dying. They seemed to think there might be a connection between that and what went down today."

"How about the guys who took the guns? Did any of them get bagged?"

"I don't know. I didn't want to probe too far, and they didn't seem willing to talk about it. The only thing they said is they were looking for a white delivery van."

Pausing, the mate looked at the chief and said, "I think we may have another problem."

"What?" the chief replied in exasperation.

"Connolly. He saw something. I don't know what or how much, but he definitely saw something. I bumped into him in the passageway when I came back aboard with the money, and he was nervous as hell. Too nervous."

"Shit!"

"Sparky is the other problem. He was supposed to be ashore. I was going to stash the money in his room in case they searched the ship. I handed the envelope to Connolly and told him to put it in Sparky's room. I went to give him the key, and he said Sparky was in his room because he heard him talking. It's my guess Connolly saw the truck and walked back past Sparky's room. In any case, he bumped into me coming out of the ladderway leading up to Sparky's deck."

"So where is the money?" the chief asked.

"I mailed it to myself in a chart tube. I had Connolly give it to the purser for the outgoing mail. It'll go ashore first thing in the morning, so we're okay there."

"Shit! Shit! Shit!" the chief muttered. "What do we do now?"

"I'm gonna have to have another talk with Connolly."

The next morning I sat and fretted, my imagination in high gear. "This is not good," I thought. "Should I come clean with the mate and tell him what I saw, or just play dumb? This is serious shit! If he thinks I'm a threat to whatever his little scam is, what could he do? What if he thinks I blew the whistle on him? What then? Fuck, fuck, fuck, fuck, fuck!"

There was a knock on my door. It opened, and the mate walked in. Normally, no one would dare to enter your room without permission. It was the only private area you had on the ship, so for the mate to just barge in gave me an indication of how uptight he was.

"We need to finish our conversation," he said.

"Look, Mate, I've been on this ship for months now, and I've seen a number of weird things. It doesn't make any difference. Whatever I saw, I've already forgotten. I don't care. It's none of my business. Not the stuff in the hatch. Not the second dying. Not Sparky getting hung up. I don't care! I just want to get on with my life."

He just stared at the deck and then looked at me.

"You said you heard Sparky talking to someone. Who was it?"

"I don't know. It was someone in his room."

"Could you hear what they were talking about?"

"All I heard was, 'You better hurry and get here.' I heard him say that for sure. I couldn't make out anything else. It sounded like he was coming out his door, so I ran out the passageway."

"Are you sure that's what you heard?"

"Yeah, I'm sure."

He stared at the deck again for what seemed forever. Then he pointed his finger at me and said, "Well, you had your chance to shoot your mouth off when the cops were here, and you didn't. If you go to them now, they'll probably think you were in on it too. Otherwise, you would have told them about it today. So you have something to lose here too."

"Mate, as far as anybody is concerned, I didn't see nothing. I don't know nothing, and that's the way it's going to stay."

"It better," he said as he turned to leave. "By the way, come to my office at 0900. The union business agent will be reviewing the work logs."

Later, in the captain's cabin, "So that's the story, Captain," the mate said. "I don't think Connolly will say anything. One, he's too scared, and two, he's a city kid and he's street smart. He knows he'd probably get dragged into it somehow, so it's in his own best interest to forget everything. I think he will. As for Sparky, no one has seen him all day. I called the union hall and asked if they had heard from him. They told me he had called and said he was getting off and they should replace him. I expect we won't see him until payoff."

"What do you think, Dennis? Did Sparky blow the whistle? God knows he hated just about everyone on this ship, especially the second engineer. We really don't know what he knew, do we?"

"No, Captain, we don't."

"All right, Dennis. Let's let sleeping dogs lie and ignore Connolly for the time being. He's a pretty good kid and has the makings of a good mate. As for Sparky, I'll talk to him at payoff and see if I can glean anything from him."

At 0900 hours I knocked on the mate's office door. "Come in," he called. Sitting in the office with him was the union business agent. The business agent said, "You got a problem."

Back when the mate had told me to cover for the second mate and given me the chart work, he had also told me to be sure the seven-day chronometers were wound. So every Saturday I faithfully wound both chronometers. What the mate didn't tell me was that, by the terms of the union contract, someone had to put in one hour's overtime every week for winding the chronometers. I didn't know it when I started doing it, but when I found out, it seemed ludicrous because it took me all of three minutes to wind both chronometers. Having come from being dead broke most of my life to now earning $30,000 a year, three times what the average college grad was making, I felt they were paying me to take an extended vacation and travel the world at their expense. So I had a hard time understanding why anyone should get paid overtime for something as simple as winding clocks, especially when there was nothing to do at sea anyway except sleep. It seemed it was abusing the privilege by putting in for it, so I didn't.

The business agent saw it differently and proceeded to rip me a new asshole and lecture me on all the benefits the early union organizers had fought so hard to get. He was right, of course. I was well aware of how difficult it used to be for crews just from the stories my old man had told me about his sailing days. But the fact that my union dues were paying his salary so he could bust my balls didn't sit well with me. Given everything else going on, I decided that eating a little humble pie was the smart thing to do, so I said, "Sorry. It won't happen again," and that was the end of it.

Chapter 34

CAPTAIN'S RECEIPTS

Sparky had slunk away from the ship after dropping a dime on the gun exchange. Worried that the chief mate or second engineer would come looking for revenge, he felt safer hiding in his father's apartment. In order to get paid, though, he had to return to the ship. Arriving at the pier at 0600 hours when no one but the gangway watchman was awake, Sparky assumed the payoff would start at 0900 hours. He was a day early. The gangway watchman, alerted the previous day to be on the lookout for Sparky, informed the chief mate, and he, in turn, told the captain, who summoned Sparky. Knocking timidly on the captain's door, Sparky walked in after hearing the captain's imperial "Enter."

"Sparky, when we were last here in Brooklyn, you said you ran into Frankie and told me he said to say hello. I know Frankie because I worked with his father for a number of years when I was the marine superintendent back in the fifties. How did you get to know him?"

"We grew up in the neighborhood here in Brooklyn together. We weren't really friends. My father ran a dry cleaning shop, and I worked there. My father had a ham radio set up in the back of the shop, and one day, when Frankie came in to pick up some clothes, he heard the squawks from the radio and asked me about it. I took him in the back and showed him the set. He got interested, asking me questions, and that's how I got to know him. The only thing we had in common was we were both ham radio operators. I ended up taking it beyond being a ham operator and made it my living. It was just a hobby for him, but we still talked occasionally on the radio."

"How often do you communicate with him?"

"Not much. When we are running the coast, I can sometimes raise him at night if the atmospherics are good. When we do talk, it's usually in Morse code." More animated, he continued, "He's pretty good at Morse code. We have a contest that's been going on for a long time now. We see who can send messages the fastest. I won most of the time but he'd occasionally beat me. But it's been a couple of years since we last talked on the radio."

"What kind of messages?"

"Oh, dumb stuff, like a famous line from a movie. Stuff like that."

"What else did you talk about with him last week?"

Looking away, Sparky stammered, "Nothing. I can't remember."

The captain stared at him and then said, "It was only last week. You can't remember what he said?"

Again Sparky mumbled, "Can't remember."

After a moment of silence, the captain said, "That's all."

Sparky got up and left the cabin.

Sitting alone in the cabin, the captain's growing suspicion changed to certainty that it was Sparky who had ratted them out to customs.

Now sitting in Lorenzo's Trattoria, a restaurant on Third Avenue, having just finished off a two-pound lobster, the captain lit up a Dunhill King-Size cigarette with his usual ritual. Even though he had sailed in and out of the Twenty-Third Street pier for many years, he had never come to this place before. Heavy red brocade covered the walls with ornate, gilt-framed paintings hung every five feet. Massive round wooden tables surrounded by captain's chairs were spaced down the left side, and a narrow bar ran down the right-hand wall. A few Roman god statues were stuck into niches and corners. The place reeked Italian motif. Turning to the man with him, the captain said, "Well, Frankie, satisfied with the 'Sapporo beer shipment'?"

"Yeah. I let the boys keep the beer after we removed the 'horse' from the cases."

"I take it, then, that the money will be showing up soon?"

"Tomorrow, same locker at Grand Central as usual. Was this your own private deal? None of your partners have a piece of it like the guns?"

The captain smiled and said, "No. All mine." After a pause, he continued, "I didn't know you were part of the gun deal."

With a slight smirk, Frankie said, "I wasn't. The fella who did the deal sent an honorarium for letting him use my pier. Sort of like rent. He was upset about customs showing up when they did. They only missed him by about a minute." Shrugging, he added, "It's the risk you take in this kind of business, but it was a little embarrassing to me. My early-warning system usually works better."

Stubbing out his half-finished smoke, the captain held out his hand and said, "It was a pleasure."

"Likewise. Dinner's on me. My cousin owns the restaurant."

"Thank you, Frankie."

As he stood, the captain looked down at Frankie, scratched his chin, and said, "Maybe your answer to your early-warning system failure can be found in Morse code. Some canaries like to sing, especially if they have a personal grudge."

Reaching across the table, Frankie grabbed the captain's hand and said, "Wait a minute! Are you telling me that little shit Sparky ratted me out on the gun deal?"

"No. He didn't rat *you* out," the captain replied, emphasizing the *you*. "I doubt he even knew you were in on it. No, he ratted out some of my partners he has a running feud with. Some of the officers didn't treat Sparky too well, and he responded in kind. But the end result is the same, isn't it?"

"Yeah, it sure as fuck is!"

"I'm sure you can clean up loose ends."

The captain walked out to Third Avenue and caught a cab back to the ship. As he settled back in the seat, he thought of his brother, Seymour, and the promise he had made to him. "Well, Seymour, your son, Sam, is gone. I can't do anything about that, but I think I've just fulfilled my last obligation to you by making sure justice is done!"

Chapter 35

SIGN OFF—PAYDAY

Sign-off day. A long time coming. All the recent tumult and anxiety were temporarily pushed aside by the excitement of going home, money in my pocket, and looking forward to seeing my buddies and flashing some green just to show them I'd turned the corner. The old days of hand-to-mouth living were gone forever!

When the purser told me the payoff was going to be delayed, something about the cash not being delivered until late afternoon, I was pissed. That meant I would miss the last shuttle to Boston and either have to stay overnight or take a bus home. The good side was, because of union rules, if the payoff wasn't completed by noon, everyone got another day's pay. I found this hilarious after just having my balls broken by the union business agent because I never put in any overtime for winding the chronometers.

Finally, around 1900 hours, the money truck showed up, and they began paying off.

Sparky, who had hidden in his room all day, wanted to be first in line. For some reason, though, the captain told him he had to wait until the unlicensed crew members were paid off. He told him to go back to his room and wait; the purser would let him know.

My pocket was burning with a little over $5,000 in cash when I signed off. Now I started to worry about going out to Third Avenue to catch a cab with that kind of money on me. The whole waterfront knew when ships got paid off, and I had already heard a few horror stories of guys getting clipped and rolled. I didn't want to rely on the fact that Frankie was my newfound friend as a deterrent to any local thugs.

While I was standing at the gangway, Sparky nearly ran me over, still whining about being practically the last one to get paid. He bounded down the gangway and ran the length of the pier, heading for the gate.

Saying good-bye to the mate, I asked, "Do you think I could get a cab to come right down to the head of the pier rather than have to walk the couple of blocks to Third Avenue?"

"At this time of night? No way! They won't even stop for you on Third Avenue if there's anyone standing around near you. If I was you, I'd stay on board tonight and leave in the morning."

This was good advice, but I was just too antsy to get going, and I only had a week before I had to rejoin the ship in Boston, so I didn't want to waste any time. I had put my money into the money belt I bought, hoping that if I were clipped, they'd only take my wallet. I kept a couple of hundred bucks in the wallet to make it look good.

When I finally walked down the gangway, it was close to 2200 hours. My knife was in a sheath on my belt, just in case.

Wired, my senses tuned in to the surroundings, I was doing fine, having passed the bar at the top of the pier, and was heading up the block. The streetlights were out, and Third Avenue was the light at the end of the tunnel. I heard scuffling sounds and stopped, my heart slamming in my chest when two guys burst out of an alley in front of me and stopped short.

"Oh shit," I thought. "Here we go."

I was deciding whether to drop my suitcase or try to hit one of them with it when the taller guy grabbed the other and said, "Let's go."

Both of them took off running toward Third Avenue.

That scared the shit out of me. Not quite believing my good luck and wanting them to get far out in front of me, I stood there for about thirty seconds. Then I heard a groan coming from the alley. Against all my instincts, I stepped into the alley and looked past the stoop leading into one of the houses. There was a body sprawled on the ground.

Constantly swiveling my head, ready to swing my suitcase if anyone came at me or came back to finish whatever they had started, I fished out my lighter and flicked it on.

Lying on the ground was Sparky, his face covered in blood. Sticking out of his chest was his own switchblade, the one he always played with. Leaning in close, I saw that there was a pink chunk, like raw meat, neatly skewered by the switchblade. It was all that remained of his tongue. The groan I heard must have been his death rattle, because he was gone. Sparky's little vendetta hadn't gone unnoticed after all.

Picking up my bag, I hurried out of the darkness of the alley and made a beeline for the lights and relative safety of Third Avenue, having learned a lesson about playing games with the wrong people. What could I look forward to on the next trip?

The End

MARITIME GLOSSARY

abeam: Direction that is at right angles to the fore-and-aft line of a ship.

able-bodied seaman (AB): Member of the deck department. Stands watches as a helmsman. Performs maintenance.

articles: A formal contract of hire between the steamship line and a crew member.

bight: A loop or slack curve in a rope or wire.

bitt: Either of a pair of posts on a ship's deck used for fastening ropes or cables, usually mooring lines.

boatswain/bosun/bo'sun: The highest-ranking unlicensed person in the deck department of a ship. Equivalent to a chief petty officer in the navy. Usually a day worker, not a watch stander.

bollard: Similar to a bitt but on the pier or dock.

burthen/athwartship: Interchangeable terms meaning side to side rather than fore and aft on a ship.

cap log: The protective barrier at the waterside edge of a pier to prevent people and things from falling into the water.

capstan: A winch, usually in the vertical axis, used for hauling ships' lines tight.

captain: Person in charge of the entire ship. Highest-ranking member of the crew.

chief engineer: Highest-ranking licensed officer in the engine department. Usually a day worker, not a watch stander.

chief mate: Highest-ranking licensed officer of the deck department. In charge of cargo operations and ship maintenance. Usually a day worker, not a watch stander.

clevis pin: A pin similar in function to a bolt.

coaming: The raised edging or border around a hatch for keeping water out.

deckie: Anyone working in the deck department of a ship, either merchant marine or navy. A term used derogatively by members of the engine department.

first engineer: Second-highest-ranking licensed officer in the engine department. Usually a day worker, not a watch stander

foc's'le: Forward-most part of the ship, used for stowage of ship's gear. Originally crew's sleeping quarters on sailing ships.

hawsepipe: The opening in a ship's bow where the anchor cable passes through.

hold: That part of a ship where cargo is stowed. The lowest level of the ship.

junior third engineer: Fifth-highest-ranking licensed officer in the engine department. Stands the eight-to-twelve sea watch.

junior third mate: Lowest-ranking licensed officer of the deck department. Stands the eight-to-twelve sea watch.

oiler: Member of the engine department. Stands sea watches and performs maintenance.

1MC: A loudspeaker communication system used on ships in the 1960s.

ordinary seaman/ordinary: Member of the deck department. Stands watches as a lookout. Performs maintenance.

pelorus: A device used in navigation for measuring the bearing of an object relative to the direction in which the ship is traveling.

RDF: Radio direction finder. A navigation instrument.

second engineer: Third-highest-ranking licensed officer in the engine department. Stands the four-to-eight sea watch.

second mate: Second-highest-ranking licensed officer of the deck department. Responsible for the navigation of the ship. Stands the four-to-eight sea watch.

snipe: Anyone working in the engine department of a ship. A term used derogatively by members of the deck department.

sounding tubes: Tubes extending from the main deck down into the lowest parts of the holds and tanks for taking soundings (reading the level of liquids).

third engineer: Fourth-highest-ranking licensed officer in the engine department. Stands the twelve-to-four sea watch.

third mate: Third-highest-ranking licensed officer of the deck department. Stands the twelve-to-four sea watch.

tweendeck: That part of a ship where cargo is stowed. Lower and upper tweendecks are above the holds and separated by hatch covers.

winch station: That area where the winch controls for the cargo fall are located.

wiper: Lowest-ranking member of the engine department. Stands sea watches and performs maintenance.

WT door: A watertight door specially designed for ships.

Walter F. Curran is a retired maritime executive living in Ocean View, DE. A member of the Rehoboth Beach Writers Guild, he has self-published a book of poetry through Amazon -*Slices of Life, Cerebral spasms of the soul* and is currently writing the second of the Young Mariner series. Readers may contact Walt via email - wfcallc@gmail.com

Made in the USA
Middletown, DE
03 September 2018